THE
VALIANT
RUNAWAYS

GERTRUDE ATHERTON

1st WORLD
LIBRARY
Literary Society

The Valiant Runaways

Gertrude Atherton

© 1st World Library – Literary Society, 2004
PO Box 2211
Fairfield, IA 52556
www.1stworldlibrary.org
First Edition

LCCN: 2004195303

Softcover ISBN: 1-4218-0134-5
Hardcover ISBN: 1-4218-0034-9
eBook ISBN: 1-4218-0234-1

Purchase *"The Valiant Runaways"*
as a traditional bound book at:
www.1stWorldLibrary.org/purchase.asp?ISBN=1-4218-0134-5

1st World Library Literary Society is a nonprofit
organization dedicated to promoting literacy by:

- Creating a free internet library accessible from any
  computer worldwide.
- Hosting writing competitions and offering book
  publishing scholarships.

Readers interested in supporting literacy
through sponsorship, donations or
membership please contact:
literacy@1stworldlibrary.org
Check us out at: www.1stworldlibrary.ORG
and start downloading free ebooks today.

The Valiant Runaways
contributed by Tim, Ed & Rodney
in support of
1st World Library Literary Society

TO

GEORGE AND GILBERT JONES
Of New York
WITHOUT WHOSE ENCOURAGEMENT THIS
YARN WOULD NEVER HAVE BEEN FINISHED

I

Roldan Castanada walked excitedly up and down the verandah of his father's house, his thumbs thrust into the red silk sash that was knotted about his waist, his cambric shirt open at the throat as if pulled impatiently apart; the soft grey sombrero on the back of his curly head making a wide frame for his dark, flushed, scowling face.

There was nothing in the surroundings to indicate the cause of his disturbance. The great adobe house, its white sides and red tiles glaring in the bright December sun, would have been as silent as a tomb but for the rapid tramping of Roldan and the clank of his silver spurs on the pavement. On all sides the vast Rancho Los Palos Verdes cleft the horizon: Don Mateo Castanada was one of the wealthiest grandees in the Californias, and his sons could gallop all day without crossing the boundary line of their future possessions. The rancho was as level as mid-ocean in a calm; here and there a wood or river broke the sweep; thousands of cattle grazed. Now and again a mounted vaquero, clad in small-clothes vivified with silver trimmings, dashed amongst tossing horns, shouting and warning.

But Roldan saw none of these things. There was reason for his disquiet. News had arrived an hour before which had thrown his young mind into confusion: the soldiers were out for conscripts, and would in all probability arrive at the Rancho Los Palos Verdes that evening or the following morning. Roldan, like all the Californian youth, looked forward to the conscription with apprehension and disgust. Not that he was a coward. He could throw a bull as fearlessly as his elder brothers; he had ridden alone at night the length of the rancho in search of a pet colt that had strayed; and he had once defended the women of the family single handed against a half dozen savages until reinforcements had arrived. Moreover, the stories of American warfare which he had managed to read, despite the prohibition of the priests, had stirred his soul and fired his blood. But army life in California! It meant languishing in barracks, hoping for a flash in the pan between two rival houses, or a possible revolt against a governor. If the Americans should come with intent to conquer! Roldan ground his teeth and stamped his foot. Then, indeed, he could not get to the battlefield fast enough. But the United States would never defy Mexico. They were clever enough for that. His anger left him, and he gave a little regretful sigh. Not only would he like that kind of a battle, but it would be great fun to know some American boys. Then he shook his head impatiently and dismissed these tourist thoughts. The present alone was to be considered.

There were two ways to avoid conscription. One was to marry - Roldan sniffed audibly; the other lay in flight and eluding the men until their round was over for the year.

Roldan did not like the idea of running away from anything; he and several of his father's vaqueros had once made an assault upon a band of cattle thieves and hunted them into the mountains: that was much more

Gertrude Atherton

to his taste. Nevertheless there was one thing he liked less than showing his heels, and that was giving up his liberty. Not to gallop at will over the rancho, or sleep in a hammock, to coliar the bulls and shout with the vaqueros at rodeo, to be the first at the games and the races, to wear his silken clothes and lace ruffles, and eat the delightful dishes his mother's cooks prepared! And then he was a very high-spirited young gentleman. Although the same obedience, almost reverence, was exacted of him by his parents that was a part of the household religion in California, yet as the youngest child, who had been delicate during his first five years, he had managed to get very badly spoiled. He did not relish the idea of leading a life of monotony and discipline, of performing hourly duties which did not suit his taste, above all of being ordered to leave his father's house as if he were a mere Indian. No, he decided, he would not go into the army - not this year nor any other year. He would defy the governor and all his men.

When Roldan made up his mind he acted promptly. No time was to be lost in this case. Now was the hour of siesta; he could have no better time to get away. A note would relieve his parents of a certain amount of anxiety; and if they did not know where he was they could not be held accountable. His blood tingled at the presentiment of the adventures he should have in that perilous journey through a country of which he knew nothing beyond his father's and the adjoining rancho. And as adventures would be but half spiced if experienced alone, he determined - and not from selfish motives only - to save his best beloved friend, Adan Pardo, from the grasp of the law likewise.

He went within and slung about himself two pistols

and a dagger. After he had made a small bundle of linen and raided the pantry, he went out to the corral, saddled his horse and packed the saddle bags, wound his lariat securely about the pommel, then galloped away on a series of adventures memorable in the annals of California.

II

Roldan's way lay over his father's leagues until two hours after nightfall. As he passed, every now and again, a herd of cattle, lounging vaqueros called to him: "Ay, Don Roldan, where do you go?" or, "The little senor chooses a hot day for his ride." But he excited no curiosity. Like all Californians he half lived in the saddle; and he was often seen riding in the direction of Don Esteban Pardo's rancho, to spend a few days with his chosen friend.

As he approached the house he saw the family sitting on the long verandah: the pretty black-eyed girls in full white gowns, their dark hair flowing to the floor, or braided loosely; Don Esteban, a silk handkerchief knotted about his head, reclining in a long chair beside his wife, a stout woman, coffee-coloured with age, attired in a dark silk gown flowered with roses. Indian servants came and went with cooling drinks. Although it was December, Winter had loitered and fallen into deeper sleep than usual on her journey South this year.

Adan was leaning against a pillar, moody and bored. He was the youngest of the boys. His brothers, elegant caballeros, who spent most of their time in the capital or on other ranches, were kind to their younger brother, but not companionable. Therefore, when Roldan galloped into sight, he gave a shout of joy and ran down the road. Roldan drew rein some distance from the house, that the conference, which must take place immediately, might be unheard by older ears.

"Listen, my friend," he said rapidly, interrupting Adan's voluble hospitality. "The soldiers are out for conscripts -"

"Ay, yi! -"

"Now listen, and don't talk until I am done. I WILL NOT be drafted as if I had no will of my own, and rot in a barrack while others enjoy life. Neither will you if you have the spirit of a Pardo and are worthy to be the friend of Roldan Castanada. So - I fly. Do you understand? - and you go with me. We will dodge these servants of a tyrant government the length and breadth of the Californias. When the danger is over for this year we will return - not before. Now, you will ask me to go to my room as soon as possible after you have given me some supper, for I am tired and want sleep. You also will take a nap. When all is quiet I shall call you and we will start."

Adan had listened to this harangue with bulging eyes and tongue rolling over his teeth. But Roldan never failed to carry the day. He was a born leader. Adan's was the will that bent; but his talent for good comradeship and his quiet self-respect saved him from servility.

In appearance he was in sharp contrast to the slender Roldan, of the classic features and fiery eyes. Short, roly-poly, with a broad, good-natured face, his attire was also unmarked by the extreme elegance which always characterised Roldan. In summer he wore

Gertrude Atherton

calico small-clothes, in winter unmatched articles of velvet or cloth, and an old sombrero without silver.

"Ay! yi!" he gasped. "Ay, Roldan! Holy Mary! But you are right. You always are. And so clever! I will go. Sure, sure. Come now, or they will think we conspire."

Roldan dismounted, and was warmly greeted by the family. The girls rose and courtesied, blushing with the coquetry of their race. Roldan cared little for girls at any time, and to-night was doubly abstracted, his ear straining at every distant hoof-beat. He retired as early as he politely could, but not to sleep. Indeed, he became so nervous that he could not wait until the family slept.

"Better to brave them, Adan," he said to his more phlegmatic friend, "than that sergeant, should he get here before we leave. Come, come, let us go."

They dropped out of the window and stole to the corral where the riding horses were kept. It was surrounded by a high wall, and the gate was barred with iron; but they managed to remove the bars without noise, saddled fresh horses and led them forth and onward for a half mile, then mounted and were off like the wind.

They knew the country down the coast on the beaten road, but they dared not follow this, and struck inland. The air was now of an agreeable warmth; the full moon was so low and brilliant that Roldan called out he could count the bristling hairs on a coyote's back.

In less than two hours they were climbing a mountain trail leading through a dense redwood forest. In these depths the moon's rays were scattered into mere flecks dropping here and there through the thick interlacing boughs of the giant trees. Those boughs were a hundred feet and more above their heads. About them was a dense underforest of young redwoods, pines, and great ferns; and swarming over all luxuriant and poisonous creepers.

They were silent for a time. The redwood forests are very quiet and awesome. At night one hears but the rush of the mountain torrent, the cry of a panther or a coyote, the low sigh of wind in the treetops.

"Ay, Roldan," exclaimed Adan, suddenly. "Think did we meet a bear?"

"We probably shall," said Roldan, coolly. "These forests have many 'grizzlies,' as the Americans call them."

"But what should we do, Roldan?"

"Why, kill him, surely."

"Have you ever seen one?"

"Never."

"But it is said that they are very large, my friend, larger than you or I."

"Perhaps. Keep quiet. I like to hear the forest talk."

"What strange fancies you have, Roldan. A forest cannot talk."

"Oh - hush."

Gertrude Atherton

"Ay, yi, Roldan! Roldan!"

The horses were standing upright, neighing pitifully. Adan gave a hoarse gurgle and crossed himself.

"The adventures have begun," said Roldan.

In a great swath of moonlight on a ledge some yards above them, standing on his hind legs and swinging his forepaws goodnaturedly, was an immense grey bear. Suddenly he extended his arms sociably, almost affectionately.

"We cannot retreat down that steep trail," said Roldan, rapidly. "He could follow faster and the horses would fall. To the left! in the brush, quick! - a bear cannot run sideways on a mountain."

The boys dug their spurs into the trembling mustangs, who responded with a snort of pain and plunged into the thicket. Only the bold skill of the riders saved them from pitching sidewise down the steep slope, despite the brush, for they were unshod and their knees had weakened.

But the grizzly, alas! was still master of the situation. In less than a moment the boys saw him lumbering along above them. He evidently had possession of a trail, more or less level.

"Dios de mi alma!" cried Adan. 'If he gets ahead of us he will come down and meet us somewhere. We shall be lost - eaten even as a cat eats a mouse, a coyote a chicken."

"You will look well lining the dark corridors of the

bear, my friend. Your yellow jacket with those large red roses, which would make a bull sweat, would hang like tapestry in the houses of Spain. Those hide boots, spotted with mud, and the blood of the calf, would keep him from wanting another meal for many a long day -"

"Ay, thou fearless one! Why, it is said that if the grizzly even raises his paw and slaps the face every feature is crushed out of shape."

"I should not be surprised."

They plunged on, tearing their clothes on the spiked brush and the thorns of the sweetbrier, fragrant lilac petals falling in a shower about them, great ferns trodden and rebounding. The air was heavy with perfume and the pungent odour of redwood and pine.

Roldan had passed Adan. Suddenly his horse stumbled and would have gone headlong had not his expert rider pulled him back on his haunches.

"What is it? What is it?" cried Adan, who also had been obliged to pull in abruptly, and who liked horses less when they stood on their hind legs. "Is it the bear upon us? But, no, I hear him - above and beyond. What are you doing, my friend?"

Roldan had dismounted and was on his hands and knees. In a half moment he stood erect.

"We are saved," he said.

"Ay? What?"

Gertrude Atherton

"It is a hole, my friend - large and deep and round. Did you put any meat in your saddle-bags?'

"Ay, a good piece."

"Raw?"

"Yes."

"Give it to me - quick. Do not unwrap it."

Adan handed over the meat, then dismounted also.

"A bear-trap?" he asked.

"Yes, a natural one. Come this way, before I unwrap the meat."

The boys forced their way to the south of the large hole, dragging the still terrified horses, who were not disposed to respond to anything less persuasive than the spur. Roldan approached the edge of the excavation and shook the meat loose, flinging the paper after it. As the smell of fresh beef pervaded the air it was greeted by a growl like rising thunder, and almost simultaneously the huge unwieldy form of the bear hurled itself down through the brush. The boys held their breath. Even Roldan felt a singing in his ears. But the grizzly, without pausing to ascertain his bearings, went down into the hole at a leap. He made one mouthful of the meat, then appeared to realise that he was in a trap. With a roar that made the horses rear and neigh like stricken things, he flung himself against the sides of his prison, drew back and leaped clumsily, tore up the earth, and galloped frantically to and fro. But he was caught like a rat in a trap.

The boys laughed gleefully and remounted their horses, which also seemed to appreciate the situation, for they had quieted suddenly.

"Adios! Adios!" cried Roldan, as they forced their way up to the trail the bear had discovered. "You will make a fine skeleton; we will come back and look at you some day."

But it was not the last they were to see of Bruin in the flesh.

Gertrude Atherton

III

An hour later they began to descend the mountain on the other side, and by dawn espied a ranch house in a valley. The white walls were pink under the first streamers of the morning. The redwoods rose like a solid black wall on the towering mountains on every side.

"Ay!" exclaimed Roldan, drawing a deep sigh. "Sleep and a hot breakfast. They will be good once more."

"They will," answered Adan, who had been collapsing and digging his knuckles into his eyes for an hour and more.

They feared that no one might be stirring, but, as they approached the verandah, the door opened and a stout smiling Californian, dressed in brown small-clothes, appeared.

"Who have we here?" he cried. "But you are early visitors, my young friends."

"We are dodging the conscript," said Roldan. "You will not betray us?"

"I should think not. I'd hide my own boys, if the mountains did not do that for me. Come in, come in.

The house is yours, my sons. Burn it if you will. Tired? Here. Go in and get into bed. The servants are not up, but I myself will make you chocolate and a tortilla."

The boys did not awaken for eight hours. When they emerged, somewhat shamefacedly, they found the family assembled on the verandah, drinking their after-noon chocolate, and impatient with curiosity. There were no girls to criticise the dilapidated garments - which the kind hostess had mended while the boys slept; but there were two youths of fourteen and fifteen and two young men who were lying in hammocks and smoking cigarritos.

Roldan and Adan were made welcome at once.

"My name is Jose Maria Perez," said the host, coming forward. "This is my wife, Dona Theresa, and these are my sons, Emilio, Jorge, Benito, and Carlos. What shall we call you, my sons?"

"My name is Roldan Castanada of the Rancho Los Palos Verdes, and this is my friend Adan Pardo of the Rancho Buena Vista."

"Ay! we have distinguished visitors. But you were just as welcome before. Sit down while I go and see if the big stew I ordered is done. Caramba! but you must be hungry."

The four lads quickly fraternised, and Roldan began at once to relate their adventures, continuing them over the steaming dish of stew. When he reached the point which dealt with the outwitting of the bear, Don Emilio sprang from his hammock.

"A bear trapped?" he cried. "A grizzly? We will have a fight with a bull. You are rested, no? As soon as you have eaten, come and show us the way."

The boys, always ready for sport, and believing that they were beyond the grasp of the law for the present, eagerly consented. An hour later Don Emilio, Don Jorge, the four lads, and three vaqueros all sallied forth to capture one poor bear. The vaqueros dragged a sled, and much stout rope.

When they reached the trap darkness had come, but the four boys held lighted torches over the hole - this was their part. The bear, disheartened with his long and futile effort to escape, lay on the uneven surface below, alternately growling and roaring. As the torches flared above him he sprang to his feet with a vast roar, his eyes as green and glittering as marsh lights. In a moment a lasso had flown over his head and he was on his back. But his formidable legs were not to be encountered rashly. Each was lassoed in turn, also his back; then his huge lunging body was dragged up the side of the excavation and onto the sled. There he was bound securely; then the rope about his neck was loosened and he was fed on a hind quarter of sheep. But it placated him little. His anger was terrific. He roared until the echoes awoke, and strained at the rope until it seemed as if his great muscles must conquer.

But he was powerless, and the procession started: first Roldan and Benito with their torches; then two vaqueros dragging the sled, the third holding the rope which encircled the bear's neck, ready to tighten it on a second's notice. Following were Don Jorge and Don Emilio, then the two other young torch bearers. Thus was poor Bruin carried ignominiously out of the forest where he had been lord, to perform for the benefit of the kind he despised. That night he rested alone in a high walled corral, liberated by the quick knife of one of the vaqueros, who sprang through the door just in time to save himself.

There was an angry guest on the ranch that night. The bear's lungs, which were of the best, had little repose, and he flung himself against the earth walls of the corral until they quivered with the impact. The horses in the neighbouring corrals whinnied; the cows in the fields bellowed. It was a vocal night, and few slept.

Nevertheless everybody was excited and good-natured next morning. Immediately after breakfast they went out to the corral, and by means of a ladder mounted the wall and stood on the broad summit. At a signal from Don Emilio a vaquero opened the gate cautiously and drove in a large bull, who had been carefully irritated since sunrise.

The two unamiable beasts, glad of an object to vent their spleen upon, flew at each other. The bear, giant as he was, was ignominiously rolled in the dust by the furious onslaught of bulk and horns. He recovered himself with surprising alacrity, however, and rushed at the bull. The latter, off guard for the moment, and struggling for his lost breath, was hurled on his back. He rolled over quickly, but before he could gather his legs under him, the bear sat himself squarely upon the heavy flanks. The bull jerked up his head, his eyes injected, his tongue rolling out. The bear raised one of his mighty paws and dealt him a box on the ear. The head fell with an ugly thud on the hard floor of the corral. The bear adjusted himself comfortably and licked his paws.

Gertrude Atherton

On the wall the onlookers were far more excited than the gladiators in the arena. The Perezes sympathised with their personal property, but Roldan and Adan felt that the bear was their menagerie, and that their honour was at stake. Party feeling ran very high. Roldan and Benito were twice separated by their anxious elders.

"Ay! yi!" cried Carlos. "The bull wakes."

The poor bull, in truth, despite the crushing weight on his vitals, raised his head again, shook himself feebly, and was once more boxed into unconsciousness. The side of his face was crushed; his body was slowly flattening. The family encouraged him with tears and spirit.

"Ay, Ignacio, Ignacio, my poor one!" cried Don Jose. "Arouse thyself and kill the brute. Ay! thou wert so beautiful, so elegant, thy sleek sides like the satin of Dona Theresa - and he like a wild man that has never washed. Where is thy pride, Ignacio? Arouse thyself!"

Thus encouraged, the bull raised his head once more. The bear gave him a whack that snapped his spinal cord, then rose and swung himself round the enclosure with the arrogant mien of a bloated sultan who has swept off a troublesome head. This attitude aroused Benito to fury.

"Ay, the cheat! the assassin!" he cried. "It was not a fair fight. Our Ignacio had no chance -"

"That is not true!" exclaimed Roldan. "He had the same chance at the first. If you are not satisfied, Senorito Benito, then fight me."

No sooner said than done. The boys, who stood some distance from the others, doubled their fists and rushed at each other like two fighting cocks. They pommelled for several minutes, then locked their arms about each other and went reeling about the wall, to the horror of the others, who dared not approach lest they should inflame them further.

"Jump down! Jump down, you imbeciles!" cried Don Jose." Do you wish to be food for the bear? A misstep - " The words ended in a hoarse gurgle. Dona Theresa shrieked. Adan and Carlos sobbed. The young men turned cold and weak. The two boys had fallen headlong into the corral.

They were sobered and fraternal in a moment. The bear stood upon his hind legs and opened his arms invitingly. He stood in front of the gate.

"Ay! ay!" gasped Benito. "He will eat us!"

"No; he will eat the bull first; but he will hug us to death - that is, if he gets us - which he won't. Adan!" he cried, "lower the ladder."

Benito began to cry, his terror enhanced by the babel of voices on the wall, each of which was suggesting a different measure. On the opposite wall and in the branches of a neighbouring tree were the Indian servants and the vaqueros. They stared stupidly, with shaking lips.

Adan had recovered his presence of mind. With a firm hand, he lowered the ladder. But his wit was not quick. He should have carried it along the wall and placed it behind the boys. Instead, it descended several yards

Gertrude Atherton

away. The bear, who appeared to be no fool, lowered his forepaws and trotted slowly toward the boys.

"Juan!" shouted Roldan to a vaquero. "Lasso the bull and drag him to the west side - far from the gate."

The vaquero, alert enough under orders, swung the lasso with supple wrist - and missed. The boys dodged the bear, who seemed in no haste, but stalked them methodically, nevertheless. The vaquero swung again. This time the rope caught the horns, was tightened by a quick turn, and the carcass went thudding across the yard. The bear gave a furious howl and plunged after. The boys scampered up the ladder. Don Jose took each by the collar and shook them soundly. When they were released they embraced each other.

"Ay! but I was inhospitable to fight my guest," sobbed Benito.

"Ay, my friend," said Roldan, with dignity, winking back the tears started by various emotions. "It is I who should have had my ears boxed by the bear for insulting my host, and bringing anguish to the house of Perez." Then he embraced Adan, but this time mutely.

Dona Theresa had been carried to her room, where she lay prostrated with a nervous headache; but her family and guests did ample justice to the chickens stewed in tomatoes, the red peppers and onions, the fried rice, tamales, and dulces which her cook had prepared in honour of the event. Excitement and good will reigned; even Don Jose had forgiven the young offenders, and they all talked at once, at the top of their voices, as fast as they could rattle and with no falling inflection. Roldan and Adan were pressed to remain at the

Hacienda Perez until the search was over, and although the former had a secret yearning for adventure he was more than half inclined to consent.

After a brief siesta the entire male population of the hacienda retired to the wall of the corral to pot the bear. It was agreed that each should fire at once, and that he who missed should have no dulces for a week.

The bear was sitting near the middle of the corral, surly but replete, for he had eaten of the bull. Don Jose gave the signal. Twenty-two shots were fired. The bear gave a roar which awoke the echoes of the forest, lunged frantically on shattered legs, then fell, an ugly heap of dusty grey hair.

As the smoke cleared and Don Jose was announcing that only two Indian servants had missed, Benito clutched Roldan's arm suddenly.

"Look up," he said. "Do you see anything? Are not those men; soldiers?"

Roldan looked up to a ledge of the high mountain before the house. A bend of the trail traversed a clearing. In this open were three men on horseback, motionless for the moment.

"Adan!" shouted Roldan. He ran down the ladder.

"I cannot be sure that those are the soldiers," he called up to Don Jose. "But I take no risks. We must go."

The others descended hastily. "My sons will have to hide too," said Don Jose. "There is plenty of time. In a moment those men will be in the forest again and can

Gertrude Atherton

see nothing more for half an hour. We must do nothing while they watch - there! they have gone."

He shouted to the vaqueros to saddle six fresh horses, and ordered the house servants to pack the bags with food.

"There is a cave in the mountain on the other side which I defy anyone to find," said Don Jose. "If there were a war my sons should fight, but I need them now."

While the horses were saddling, Roldan and Adan consulted together. At the end of a few moments the former went up to Don Jose.

"I think it would be wiser to separate," he said. "Adan and I will go one way, your sons another. That will put them off the track; and the cave, Carlos says, is not very large."

"As you like," said Don Jose, who was perturbed and busy. "A vaquero will go with you for a distance and advise you."

The truth was, Roldan fancied lying inert in a cave for several days as little as he fancied the somnolent life of a barrack, and Adan, who had a secret preference for the cave, was too loyal to oppose him.

In ten minutes the horses were ready, affectionate good-byes said, and Roldan and Adan, followed by many good wishes, and prayers to return, started southeastward through a dense canon.

IV

The vaquero guided the boys rapidly through the
canon. The almost perpendicular walls, black with a
dense growth of brush and scrub trees, towered so high
above them that the atmosphere was damp and the long
strip of sky was like a pale-blue banner. The trail was
well worn, and there was nothing to impede their
progress. The mustangs responded to the lifted bridle
and ran at breakneck speed. They emerged at the end
of half an hour. It was an abrupt sally, and the great
level plain before them seemed a blaze of sunlight.

"Bueno," said the vaquero, halting. "Ride straight
ahead. Keep to the trail. At night you will come to a
river. Before you reach it all trace of you will be lost,
because between now and there are many side trails,
and as the ground is so hard they cannot tell which you
take. Cross the river and take the trail to the left. That
will bring you to the Mission - about twenty miles
farther - where the good padres will let you rest and
give you fresh horses. The senor, meanwhile, will
throw the officers off the scent. But if you are wise,
you will make for the Sierras and hide there. Adios,
senor, adios, senor;" and he wheeled about and
disappeared into the darkness of the canon.

"We are like the babes in the wood," said Adan. "I feel
as if we never should find our way home again."

Gertrude Atherton

"We shall," said Roldan, stoutly; although he, too, felt the chill of the immense solitude. "And we have begun well! What an adventure to start with! I am sure we shall have more."

Adan crossed himself.

The boys rode at a long even gallop, the high chaparral closing behind them. Every half hour they paused, and Roldan, dismounting, held his ear to the ground. But as yet they were unpursued.

A soft wind blew over the plain, fragrant with the honeydew of the chaparral. The sun set in a great bank of yellow cloud. Then the night came suddenly.

A few moments later Roldan called: "Halt!" and held up his hand. "I hear the rush of the water," he said. "We must be near the river."

"It sounds as if it was high," said Adan. "It has rained hard this month. Suppose these horses don't swim?"

"We'll make them. Come on."

"Ay! yi!" exclaimed Adan, not many moments after.

They pulled up suddenly on the banks of the river, a body of water about three hundred yards wide. It was swollen almost level with the high banks. The tumultuous waters were racing as if Neptune astride them was fleeing from angry gods. There is something unhuman in the roar of an angry river: it has a knell in it.

Roldan and Adan looked at each other. The latter's face

had paled. Roldan contracted his lids suddenly, and when his friend met the glance that grew between them he compressed his lips and involuntarily straightened himself: he knew its significance.

"We must cross," said Roldan. "It would never do to spend the night on this side. If they followed, they would never suspect us of crossing. If we remained here, we could not hear them until they were upon us."

"Very well," said Adan.

Roldan raised his bridle. The mustang did not move forward, but cowered. "I don't like to hurt horses," said the young don, "but he's got to go." He clapped his spurs savagely against the animal's sides, and the next moment the waves were lashing about him.

Adan was beside him at once, and together they breasted the rushing waters. The mustangs were strong and made fair headway, incited by terror and the spur. The water was very cold, but the boys scarcely felt it. Their eyes were strained toward the opposite shore, measuring the distance, which seemed to grow less very slowly. The stars were thick and the moon was floating just above the chaparral, but the darkness about them was grim, and only a narrow line of white indicated the shore.

The horses were not able to keep a straight course. The current lashed them about more than once, but they righted, shook the water from their quivering nostrils, and plunged on.

The boys' glance so persistently sought their haven that they saw nothing of what was passing about them.

　　　　Gertrude Atherton

They were within twenty yards of the shore. Adan, having the stronger beast, was some little distance ahead. He did not observe it. He was registering a vow that if he reached land in safety he would be drafted every year of his life before he would ford another river after heavy rain.

Suddenly Roldan became conscious that the wiry little body between his gripping knees had relaxed somewhat the tension of its muscles. Was the poor brute collapsing? Roldan leaned over and patted his neck. It responded for a moment, then fell back again. Roldan set his lips. As he did so he cast about him the instinctive glance of those in peril. A huge log was bearing down upon him like a projectile.

In a second his feet were out of his stirrups and he was crouching on the mustang's back. The log struck the beast full in the side, tossing Roldan as if he had been a feather. The mustang gave a hoarse neigh, unheard above the roar of the water.

Roldan, keeping his face from the pounding waves as best he could, struck out for the bank. But the current was too much for his slender body, plucky as it was. He made a mighty effort and shouted, -

"Adan!"

The high clear note pierced to his companion's ear. Adan turned his head, uttered a cry, and pulled his unwilling mustang about. But the current was carrying the white face on the waves rapidly past.

"Lariat!" Roldan managed to scream.

Adan's faculties had been paralysed for the moment, but they responded almost automatically to that imperious will. He unwound the lariat rapidly from the pommel, hastily gathered the loops, then flung it with sure hand straight at his friend. It fell about Roldan's neck. The boy jerked it over his shoulders, then signed to Adan to proceed.

Adan once more urged his horse forward, not daring to look behind. Roldan made no attempt to swim; he merely used his arms to keep his head above water. There were but a few yards farther. The mustang, despite his double load, made them, and scrambled up the bank. Adan, realising for the first time that he was stiff with cold, scrambled off and pulled in the rope with hands that were aching and almost numb. He heard Roldan strike the bank, a moment later the snapping of brush. Roldan's head rose into view, Adan gave a last despairing tug, and a moment later the two boys lay on their backs, panting for breath.

Gertrude Atherton

V

"Do you want any more adventures?" asked Adan feebly, after a time.

"Not at present," said Roldan.

He raised himself stiffly. "Come," he said, "this will never do. We shall both have rheumatism. We must have a fire at once."

Adan groaned pathetically, but got on his feet. They had found refuge in the open; but a grove of trees was near, and in a quarter of an hour they had piled a heap of branches and chaparral as high as an Indian pyre, hunted up two pieces of flint, and sent sparks flying through the dry mass.

The boys divested themselves of their dripping clothes and hung them close to the fire, then raced up and down with what energy was left in them to scotch the chill night air. Finally they paused breathless before the pile, which was now roaring merrily.

"I should like to know what we are to have for supper," said Roldan. "That Mission is twenty miles away, and I for one can't walk to it. Climb up a tree and see if there is a light anywhere."

"Thanks, senor," said Adan, "when my clothes are dry."

"True, we must keep our skin. I have it!" He sprang on the back of the mustang, who also had fallen upon reaching the shore but had risen to nibble for supper, and stood on the tips of his feet. "I can see well," he announced. "But all the same I can see nothing. We must stay here."

He dismounted, and relieving the mustang of the heavy saddle, emptied the bags. "The bread and sweets are soaked," he said, "not fit for a pig to eat; but we can do something with the meat. Fetch some coals."

Adan with infinite difficulty managed to scrape a few coals apart from the bonfire, and over this they scorched the meat. As they crouched on the ground they looked like two little white savages, and they were neither comfortable nor happy.

"We must keep this fire going all night," said Roldan, "or we shall be eaten by bears, to say nothing of rattlesnakes -"

"Hist!" whispered Adan. "I hear one." Both boys sprang to their feet.

"Where?"

"Near the horse."

Roldan seized his pistol and ran in the direction indicated, keeping his eyes on the ground. Suddenly he paused. Something just beyond the light was growing into a series of graceful loops. A long neck slowly lifted itself and two baleful eyes fixed upon Roldan. He raised his pistol, and the rattler was beheaded as neatly as if it were stuffed and dismembered with a pen knife. It shot out to full length, and the clever marksman took it by its horny tail and dragged it to the fire.

"He didn't know that we'd have him for supper," said Adan, gleefully. "Here, let us eat our steak and then I'll skin him."

The steak proved tough, and when it had been disposed of with many grumblings, the rattlesnake was skinned and roasted, and proved very delicate and edible.

"Now," said Roldan, "we must sleep." Their clothes being dry they dressed; and after inspecting with a torch a circle of about two hundred yards to see that there were no snake holes, they built a hasty ring of chaparral, set fire to it that beasts and reptiles should keep their distance, then lay down and slept. Roldan was always a light sleeper, and with the fire on his mind awoke every few hours and gathered fresh chaparral or roused the heavier Adan. Coyotes wailed in the distance, and once as Roldan gathered brush he heard again the deadly rattle. But they were not disturbed, and even the skies were kind, for although clouds gathered, they passed.

They awoke in the morning, fresh and vigorous - but also hungry; and there was little to eat.

"I don't think I should fancy rattlesnake for breakfast," said Roldan, and Adan shuddered at the mere thought. They cooked a small piece of meat, all that was left of their store, and it but whetted their appetite.

"There's only one thing to do," said Roldan, "and that is to get to the Mission as quickly as possible. Chocolate! Beans! possibly chicken! Think of it. Come! Come!"

Adan scrambled to his feet and saddled the mustang. It was agreed that they should ride him by turns, the other running at a brisk trot.

The sun was barely up when they started. A light mist lay on the turbulent waters and puffed among the sweet-scented chaparral. Roldan rode during the first hour, Adan running ahead, his glance darting from right to left, but encountering eyes neither malignant nor savage. Shortly after he mounted the horse the mist lifted and rolled back to the ocean. They had left the chaparral some time before and now discovered that they were in an open plain. In the distance were high hills over which wound a white trail. Between these hills and the travellers was a moving mass of something. Adan reined in suddenly.

"Roldan," he said, "are those horses? You have the longer sight."

Roldan made a funnel of his hand. "Surely, surely!" he cried. "What luck! I hate walking. They are probably wild, but I never saw the mustang I could not lasso."

"Yes, you can do the lassoing," said Adan, grimly. "My thumb nearly went off last night, and is twice its size."

"Adan," said his friend, laying his hand on his comrade's knee. "I haven't thanked you. I haven't mentioned it; but it is because - well - I lay awake an hour last night trying to think of something to say - and - and - thinking that I loved you better than my own brothers -"

"That will do, then," said Adan, gruffly. "We'll be kissing each other in a minute as we did at the Hacienda Perez; and I think that we are getting too big for that. I hear that American boys never kiss each other."

"Don't they?" asked Roldan, pricking up his ears. "How I should like to know some American boys. They must know so many things that we do not. Who told you?"

"Antonio Scarpia has been in America, you know - in Boston. He came back last month and rode over a few days ago for the night. I asked him many questions. He says they never show any feeling except when they get mad, and that they walk and row and play ball - with the feet, caramba! - and run about in the snow. He says they would think we were like girls with our fine clothes and our hammocks -"

"Girls!" cried Roldan, indignantly. "I'd like to see American or any other boys do better with that bear than we did, or lasso a friend in the midst of a boiling river as you did. And if they come here to laugh at us they'll find one pair of fists that are not soft if they do have lace ruffles over them. And I'd like to see them live all day on a horse as we do."

"True, true, you are always right," said Adan, soothingly. "Ay, I think those horses are coming this way. Better get up."

He moved back onto the anquera and Roldan sprang to his place and unwound the lariat. Like all of its kind, it was a slender woven cord about eighteen feet in length and made of tough strips of untanned hide. It was an admirable weapon in skilled hands, but not to be trifled with by the amateur. Many a careless Californian had lost a finger or thumb, and more than one had owed it lockjaw.

The wild horses advanced rapidly for a time, but when they saw that the brother to which curiosity had attracted them was apparently of an eccentric build they suddenly paused and scattered. Roldan raised the bridle and dashed in pursuit; but the others were unincumbered, fleet of foot and terrified. They fled like the wind.

"Drop off!" commanded Roldan, reining in. "Quick! I WILL have one."

Adan slid to the ground and the mustang sprang lightly forward. Roldan had singled out a well-built black, a little heavier than his mates and consequently some-what in their rear. The mustang, who had slept off his fatigue, had no need of spur; he seemed to enter into the spirit of the chase - possibly realised that if the chase failed he might have a double load to carry. He dashed over the rough adobe plain, Roldan holding the bridle high in his left hand, the coiled lasso in his right. Adan waddled after, far in the rear. The other horses had fled to the four winds, but the pursued, occasionally ducking his head and kicking up his hind legs as if in contempt of the pretensions of mere man, made straight for the hills. Being undisciplined, however, he got over the ground clumsily, stumbled once or twice in the wide cracks of the adobe soil, and finally stopped short for want of wind. He swung about and glared defiantly at his pursuers out of injected eyes. He had never seen a lasso before, possibly not a man; but his instinct told him that the horse and rider behind him were not roving the plain in his own aimless fashion. He stood pawing the ground and shaking his great red nostrils. Suddenly to his surprise the part of the horse new to him lifted itself, and a black coiling something, graceful and swift as a rattlesnake, sprang through the air with a sharp audible rush. A quarter of a moment later he neighed with rage and terror: his neck was in a vice.

He gave a leap that nearly dragged Roldan from his saddle; but that expert young gentleman had secured the lariat to the high pommel of his saddle in a trice, and Don Jose Perez's mustang had thereafter to bear the brunt of the strain.

The wild animal pulled and tugged and tore up the ground; but finding that he but increased his own discomfort, he gradually subsided, and when Roldan finally turned about and rode slowly toward Adan he followed meekly enough.

When Adan saw the procession start in his direction he sat down on a stone to rest, and when it reached him he obeyed orders and sprang on the mustang's back as Roldan slipped off.

"That was well done, my friend." he said approvingly. "I could see it all; but I thought my eyes would fly out of my head."

Roldan walked cautiously up to his prize and attempted to pat it gently on the head. But it was some moments before he was able to touch the beast, who was sulky, cross, and frightened. When he did he swiftly loosened the lariat, and this procured him a meed of favour. The horse then allowed himself to be patted all down the side and back, nor once raised his hoof.

Suddenly Roldan sprang to his back, gripping the mane with his hands, the flanks with his knees. But this was one liberty too much. The horse stood on his hind legs, made as if to go over backward, then suddenly stiffened all four legs and sprang up and down as automatically as if worked by a spring. Roldan was now in his element. He had broken in more than one bucking horse. He remained as immovable as a fly on the top of a coach, only giving an occasional prick with his spur to madden the animal and wear him out the sooner.

Roldan had cast the lariat from the animal's neck as soon as he mounted, and it was well that he had, for his quarry made a sudden dash and did not stop for half a mile, - when he paused on his forefeet, waving his hind in the air.

But still Roldan kept his seat, Adan shouting: "Bravo! Bravo!" by way of encouragement.

The battle lasted nearly an hour; then the mustang confessed himself conquered, and the boys sought out the trail, from which they had wandered far, and continued their journey.

"Caramba!" exclaimed Roldan, "but I am famished, not to say tired. If it had been ten miles instead of twenty, it would not have been worth while."

VI

They rode on rapidly, too hungry to talk. The ground
began to rise, and they advanced through hills
sprouting with the early green of winter. Once they
paused, and tethering the horses where they could feed,
shot several quail and roasted them. But the pangs of
hunger were by no means allayed, and when, in the
early afternoon, they saw the white walls of the
Mission below them, they gave a shout of joy.

The Mission stood in the middle of a valley, well away
from woods and hills, and surrounded by a large
vineyard and orchard. On the long corridor traversing
the building adjoining the church, several figures in
habit and cowl walked slowly behind the arches.
Indians were in the vineyards and orchards and moving
about the rancheria adjacent to the main buildings.
Cattle were browsing on the hills. A stream tangled in
willows cut a zig-zag course across the valley.

The boys rode quickly down the hillside. As the padres
heard the approaching hoof-beats they paused in their
walk, and shading their eyes with their hands gazed
earnestly at the travellers.

"Friends! Friends!" cried Roldan gaily, as the tired
steeds trotted up to the corridor. The boys dismounted
and made a deep reverence. One of the priests, a man

with a grave stern face came forward.

"Who are you, my children?" he asked. "You are the sons of aristocrats, and yet you are torn and unkempt, and one of you has ridden many leagues without a saddle. Are you runaways? The shelter of the Mission is for all, but we do not countenance insubordination."

Roldan introduced himself and his friend. "We are runaways, my father," he added, "but from the government; and we have arranged that our parents shall not be anxious. We do not wish to be drafted."

The priest's brow relaxed. The padres had little respect for a system that owed its existence mainly to the vanity of governors and generals, and the present governor, Micheltorena, had by no means won the approval of the Church.

"You are welcome, my sons," he said. "If the officers come we cannot deny your presence; but I do not think they will find their way here, and we certainly shall not send for them. You are hungry and tired, no?"

"Father, we could eat our horses."

The padre laughed, and calling a young brother who was piously telling his beads bade him go and see that a hasty luncheon was prepared. An Indian came and took the mustangs, and the boys were led by the hospitable priest into a large room, comfortably furnished, the walls hung with some very good religious pictures.

The padres, in truth, were glad of visitors at any time. They were clever educated men who had given their

lives to christianising brainless savages in a sparsely
settled country; and any news of the outer world was
very welcome. They pushed back their hoods and sat
about the boys, their faces beaming with interest and
amusement as they listened to the adventures of those
wayward youths. And as all men, even priests, love
courage and audacity, they clapped their hands
together more than once or embraced the lads heartily.

When luncheon was announced and the doors of the
long refectory thrown open, the boys were shown in as
if they had been princes and told to satisfy themselves.
This they did, nor ever uttered a word. The priests had
tactfully withdrawn. Roldan and Adan ate enough
beans, rice, cold chicken, tongue, and dulces to make
up for their prolonged fast, and finished with a cup of
chocolate and a bunch of grapes. After that they went
to sleep in two clean little cells, to which they were
conducted, nor awakened until all the air was ringing
with the sweet-voiced clangor of mission bells.

Roldan turned on his elbow and looked out of the
window. The square was rapidly filling with Indians,
some running in willingly enough, others driven in at
the end of the leash by the lay brethren. All knelt on
the ground for a few moments. Roldan, whose eyes
were very keen, and, during these days, preternaturally
sharpened, noted that several of the Indians were
whispering under cover of the loud mutterings about
them. The face of the Californian Indian is not pleasant
to contemplate at any time: it is either stupid or
sinister. Roldan fancied he detected something particularly evil in the glance of the whispering savages,
and resolved to warn the priests.

The scene was peaceful enough. The cattle browsing

on the hills gave the landscape an air of great repose, and the mountains beyond were lost under a purple mist. The large stone fountain in the court splashed lazily. As the worshippers rose and withdrew, the silver bells rang out a merry peal, announcing that the morrow would be Sunday.

Roldan fell asleep again. When he awoke it was dark outside, but on the table by his cot was a lighted taper and a dish of fruit. He ate of the fine grapes and pears, then rose and opened his door. In the small room beyond a young priest was seated at a table, bending over a large leaf of parchment, to which he was applying a pen with quick delicate strokes. He looked up with a smile.

"What are you doing?" asked Roldan, curiously, approaching the table.

"Illuminating the manuscripts of a mass. Look." And he displayed the exquisite border to the music, the latter written with equal precision and neatness. "This will be alive when I am not even dust. No one will know that I did it; but I like the thought that it may live for centuries."

"If I did it, I should sign my name to it," said Roldan, with his first prompting of ambition. "But I never could do that; I have not the patience. I mean to be governor of the Californias."

"I hope you may be," said the young priest, gravely.

"Are all your Indians docile?" asked Roldan, abruptly.

The priest raised his head. "Why do you ask?"

Roldan related his suspicions.

The priest shot a furtive glance through the open window at the dark square.

"I don't know," he said slowly. "Sometimes I have thought - you see, many are stubborn and intractable, and have to be flogged and chained. Privately I think we are wasting our energies. We will leave California several beautiful monuments for posterity to wonder at, but as for the Indians we will end where we began. They are always escaping and running back to the mountains. Their every instinct is for barbarism; they have not one for civilization, nor can any be planted whose roots will not trail over the surface. The good Lord intended them to be savages, nothing more; and it is mistaken sentimentalism - However, it is not for me to criticise, and I beg, Don Roldan, that you will not repeat what I have said."

"Of course I shall not; but tell me, do you think there is danger?"

"We have one rather bright young Indian - there are about a dozen exceptions in all California, and they are treacherous. His name is Anastacio, and he has great influence with the other Indians. A good many of them are angry at present because they have been punished for stealing grapes and stores, and just now they are rather excited because it has been proposed to banish Anastacio to a Mission where there are more soldiers, - he is regarded as the inciter of the outrages."

"Have you soldiers here?"

"Eleven. The guard house is in the left hand corner of

the square. But what could they do in an uprising? We must get rid of Anastacio. I will go now and speak to Padre Flores."

Roldan went out into the square and strolled over to the soldiers' quarters. The door was closed, but light streamed from an uncovered window, and he had a good view of the guard room. A half dozen soldiers were lying about on benches, half-dressed, smoking the eternal cigarrito. Two were at a table writing. None looked alert, but as Roldan passed out of the plaza to the open beyond, he encountered a sentinel who was ready to gossip with the young don and told him that three more were on duty on the several sides of the square.

Roldan strolled on to the rancheria, a collection of six or eight hundred huts of mud and straw among a thicket of willows by the creek. Here all was dark and quiet. He glanced through several of the uncurtained windows and saw whole families peacefully asleep. Suddenly he paused and held his breath, at the same time retreating into the heavy shade of a willow. A number of doors had opened almost simultaneously; there was the sharp crunch of dry brush, and dark figures glided, with the snake-like motion peculiar to the Indian, toward the upper end of the rancheria.

Roldan waited a moment, then followed softly. He had set himself the duty of saving the Mission which had shown him hospitality, and was not to be deterred. Moreover, the spirit of adventure was by no means quenched.

In a few moments he paused opposite a large hut, from which issued a subdued murmur. The window had

Gertrude Atherton

been covered, but a thin ray of light pierced through a crack in the door, and to this Roldan applied his eye.

The room was crowded with Indians standing respectfully about a man in the middle of the room, whom Roldan knew instinctively to be Anastacio. He was big and clean-limbed and sinewy, with small cunning eyes, a resolute mouth and chin, and an air of perfect fearlessness. Roldan warmed to him, and looked with admiration and envy at the muscles on his splendid limbs.

He was speaking rapidly in the native patois, and Roldan could gather little of his meaning beyond what his gestures conveyed. He shook his fist in the direction of the Mission, snapped his fingers in scorn, pointed toward the mountains, then made the motion of speeding an arrow from the bow, at the same time contracting his face hideously.

Roldan stayed as long as he dared, then returned hastily to the Mission. A friar was locking up for the night, and began to chide the young guest for being out so late, but Roldan interrupted him impatiently.

"Can I see Padre Flores to-night?" he asked. "I must see him. It is important."

"He has retired to his cell, but I will take your message; and he never denies himself to those that need him."

He went to the end of the corridor and tapped at a door. In a few moments he returned.

"Padre Flores will see you," he said.

The priest was standing by the little altar in the corner of his cell when Roldan entered.

"What is it, my son?" he asked. "Have you learned anything new? Padre Estenega has told me of your suspicions."

Roldan rapidly related what he had seen. The priest's face became grave and anxious.

"There is trouble brewing, I fear," he said. Then he smiled suddenly. "You ran away to avoid fighting. It would be odd if you found yourself in the midst of it."

"I did not run away to avoid fighting," said Roldan, flushing hotly. "Pardon, father; I meant that you have misunderstood. I do not choose to be shut up in a barrack against my will, but I am ready to fight; and, although I am not yet sixteen, you shall see that I can help you protect your Mission. And Adan too."

"I am sure of it. I did but tease you. And your part shall begin to-night. You are rested, no?"

"I feel as if I wanted no more sleep for a week."

"Very well. Tell brother Antonio - whom you met on the corridor just now - to let you in the church by the side door and give you the key, with which you will lock yourself in. Then go up into the belfry and watch. It is the full of the moon and clear. If you merely see a dozen or more figures gliding about the rancheria, that will mean that they are plotting, and intend no action to-night. If you see several hundred, run down and bring me word. But if you see a mass of men rise at once and descend upon the west gate, ring the bells. I

Gertrude Atherton

shall go and warn the soldiers, and every priest and brother will sleep on his pistol to-night. But I don't think they are organised as yet. Before dawn I shall send a messenger to the nearest town for reinforcements. Go, my son. You are a brave and clever lad."

Roldan ran down the corridor and secured admission to the church. When he had locked the door behind him, the vast dark building, beneath whose tiles priests lay buried, shook his spirit as night and the plains had not done, and he wished that he had brought Adan. Then he jerked his shoulders, reflected that cowards did not carry off the prizes of the world, and determined that his first should be the admiration and approval of the priests and soldiers of this great Mission. He walked rapidly down the nave, trying not to hear the hollow echo of his footsteps, then opened several doors before he found the one behind which was the spiral stair leading to the belfry. His supple legs carried him swiftly up the steep ascent, and in a moment he was straining his eyes in the direction of the rancheria.

The belfry was about ten feet square. The massive walls contained three large apertures, through which the clear sonorous notes of the great bells carried far. Just beneath the arch Roldan had selected as observatory, and on the side opposite the plaza was the private garden of the padres, surrounded by cloisters. An aged figure, cowled, his arms folded, was pacing slowly.

Roldan, glancing over his shoulder, saw Padre Flores return from the soldiers' quarters; but in the rancheria there was no motion but the swaying tops of the willows, and no sound anywhere but the hoot of the owl and the yap of the coyote.

It was a long and lonely watch. Roldan felt as if he were suspended in air, cut off from Earth and all its details. Although his military instinct had been aroused and he burned for fight, his spirit grew graver in that isolation, and he resolved to do all he could to save the Mission from attack. It was there for peace and good deeds, and its preservation was of far more importance than a small pair of spurs for Master Roldan.

Nevertheless, Roldan was to win his spurs.

Toward morning he saw an Indian, attended by a priest, let himself out of a gate and steal toward the corral. A few moments later he reappeared, leading a mustang up the valley in the shadow of the trees. The priest re-entered the gate, and Roldan knew that the messenger had gone forth for help.

At sunrise a brother came running up the stair. "Better go down," he said, smiling. "I am going to ring for mass, and it will deafen you. You saw nothing, of course?"

"Nothing."

"We did not expect it, and slept. It takes time to organise."

"Have they any weapons?"

"Their bows and arrows. We have always thought it best to leave them those in case of assault by savage tribes."

Roldan descended the stair as the bells rang out their peremptory summons. Although he was tired and sleepy, he determined to remain in the church during mass, and knelt near the altar by a pillar where he could command a view of the nave. Almost the first to enter was Anastacio. He carried himself proudly - like a warrior, thought Roldan - and advancing to the altar bowed low, then knelt stiffly, his eyes closed.

The others drifted in slowly: the women kneeling on the right, the men on the left. Finally all the priests and brothers, except Padre Flores, who conducted the service, entered and knelt in the aisle. Padre Flores' garments were as rich as any worn in old Spain, and the candelabra about him were as massive. The images of the saints were clad in white satin embroidered with gold and silver thread. On the walls were many high-coloured paintings of saints, softened by the flood of light from the wax candles.

Roldan watched keenly all the faces within the line of his vision. They were mostly sleepy. Suddenly, as his glance shifted, it encountered the eyes of Anastacio. Those powerful crafty orbs were fixed upon him under drawn brows.

"He suspects me," thought Roldan, and then once more demonstrated that several of his talents were diplomatic. He glanced past the Indian indifferently to the women, then to the priests, and from there to the paintings and altar, his regard but that of the curious traveller.

When Roldan left the church he encountered Adan, who evidently had entered last and knelt near the door.

"Where did you go last night?" Adan demanded loudly.

"I sat up talking to the priests and roaming about the square," replied Roldan. Anastacio was almost at his elbow.

"Well, I had had sleep enough by twelve o'clock and I went into your cell, and then spent the rest of the night waiting for you to come back."

"I hope breakfast is ready. Come."

They went to the refectory, where Padre Flores embraced Roldan heartily, but made no allusion to his watch; there were Indian servants present. After breakfast the two boys walked up and down the middle of the square, and Roldan related his experience of the night. Adan listened with open mouth and shortened breath.

"Caramba!" he ejaculated. "Is there to be a fight?"

"I am sure of it. Are you frightened?"

"Not I. I'd rather fight Indians than ford a river. But do you think we can hold out?"

"We can try. And if they don't make the attack to-night, we shall have the better chance, because the reinforcement will arrive to-morrow. But that Anastacio suspects me, and doubtless he has discovered in some way that the messenger has gone. I am sure there will be trouble to-night, and I am going now to get a good sleep. Do you sleep, too; and see that you eat no dulces for supper, lest they make you heavy."

He awoke about four in the afternoon. There was a babel of voices in the plaza, and he sprang out of bed, excited with the thought that war had begun. But he saw only a typical Mission Sabbath afternoon. Several hundred Indians were seated on the ground in groups of two or three, gambling furiously. Through the open gates opposite, Roldan could see a spirited horse-race, a crowd of Indians betting at the top of their voices.

Roldan went to the kitchen and asked for a cold luncheon, then sought Padre Flores. The priest was in his cell, and as he saw Roldan he motioned to him to close the door.

"I can learn nothing, my son," he said; but something in the air tells me that there will be trouble to-night. Will you watch again?"

"I will, my father."

"We will all sleep on our pistols. Now listen. All we can do is to protect the gates. If you ring once that means that the Indians are advancing on the south gate, the one nearest the rancheria. But they are crafty, and will doubtless seek to enter by one less guarded. Two peals will mean the west gate, three the east, and a wild irregular clamour the north. Can you remember?"

"I can, my father," said Roldan, proudly.

"I believe you. Go up into the tower at sundown, which is the hour when the gates are closed. As soon as you have finished ringing you can come down and join in the fight. The arms will be kept in the room where we sat yesterday until your meal was made ready. Now go, my son, and God bless you. Ah!" he called after him. "Wait a moment. Get a cassock and put it on. It will make you shapeless among the bells. Otherwise you might be seen."

Roldan was at his post as soon as the Indians had been driven through the gates for the night. They straggled about the valley, still talking excitedly; but there was nothing unusual in this, the watcher had been told. Gradually they moved toward the rancheria, disappeared into it, and the valley was as quiet as it had been the night before.

In the great court there were rifts of light at irregular intervals; the heavy wooden shutters of every window were ajar. Roldan felt the nervous tension of those minds below, and with it a sense of companionship, very different from the oppressive loneliness of his previous watch.

The clock of the Mission had just struck eleven when Roldan stood suddenly erect and hooped his hands about his eyes. Something was moving in the willows beside the river. The moon shone full on the rancheria, and when the outer edge of the latter appeared to broaden and project itself the effect was noticeable at once.

Roldan watched breathlessly. In a moment there could no longer be any doubt: a broad compact something was moving down the valley toward the Mission. And an army of cats could not have made less sound.

He laid his hand on the bell rope. The Indians came swiftly, but their course was not yet defined. When within a hundred yards of the Mission they deflected suddenly to the right. Their destination was not the south gate.

Roldan closed his eyes for a half moment to relieve them of the strain, then opened them and held his breath. Only the outer fringe of the little army could now be seen; it was crawling close to the western wall. In a few moments they were beneath Roldan; he could hear the slight impact with the air. Then once more he strained his eyes until he thought they would fly from his head, and his lungs seemed bursting. They were approaching the west gate.

They passed it. There could be no doubt now that they purposed to attack the north gate; but Roldan dared not ring until they were well away from the west side, lest they change their plans and his signal mislead.

As they reached the corner of the wall they suddenly accelerated their pace as if impatience mastered them. When the tail of the procession had whisked about and Roldan saw a compact mass move like a black cloud before the wind toward the north gate, he caught the rope in both hands and jangled with all his might.

The great clapper hurled itself against the mighty sides of the bell with a violence which split the nerves and made the ear-drums creak. The blood surged to Roldan's head, carrying chaos with it. He had a confused sense of a flood of light in the plaza below, but could hear no other sound except the deafening uproar in his ears. Suddenly something gave way beneath his feet. He had an awful feeling of disintegration, of solid parting from solid in empty space. He kicked out wildly. His feet touched nothing. Then his head suddenly cleared, although the deep tones of the bell still seemed echoing there, and he became aware that his descent had stopped, and that his hands, torn and aching, were still clutching the rope. He knew what had happened. He had stepped too far and gone through one of the arches.

There was no time for fright. He began to pull himself up by the rope, hand over hand. At the same time he was acutely conscious of many things. The Indians were yelling like demoniacs and battering at the gate. In the garden on the other side, the old priest was shouting Ave Marias in a high quavering voice. A breeze had sprung up and Roldan felt the chill in it. And he felt the weight of the cassock. The heavy woollen garment fatigued his arms and impeded his progress. Were it not for that he could scramble up like a monkey.

He was within two feet of the top. Suddenly he felt a slackening of the rope, accompanied by a faint sickening sound. The rope was old, it was giving way.

Roldan made a wild lurch for the projecting floor of the belfry. The rope broke. He went down.

He had heard that a drop, however swift, might seem to occupy hours to the doomed. To his whirling horror-struck brain this descent certainly seemed very long. It was almost as if he were sauntering. Nor was he tumbling over and over. He had shut his eyes tight when the rope snapped. He opened them, gave a shuddering glance downward, then laughed almost hysterically: his cassock, ample even for a man, had caught the breeze and spread out on all sides like a parachute.

And although the descent occupied but a moment longer, he comprehended the situation, with his abnormally sharpened senses, as clearly as though he

Gertrude Atherton

stood on high with a spy glass.

All the inhabitants of the Mission proper - the priests, brothers, soldiers, and house servants - were standing before the north gate, firearms in hand. Beyond were some twenty-five Indians battering and yelling, making noise enough to induce the belief that they numbered ten times as many more. The rest were not to be seen, but it was not difficult for Roldan to suspect their purpose.

He lighted on the stone steps of the church, tore off his heavy garment, and ran toward the north gate. As he did so the east gate fell with a crash, and five hundred Indians rushed into the plaza.

They uttered no sound. The guard at the upper end of the square was not aware of their advent until Roldan reached them. He was out of breath, but he caught the arm of the man nearest him and pointed. In a second the word had passed, and the handful of defendants stared helplessly at the advancing hordes. But only for a moment. Padre Flores shouted to fall into line, then ordered them not to fire in the same breath. Anastacio, somewhat ahead of his followers, was approaching with a white rag in his hand.

When within a yard of the missionaries he paused and saluted respectfully.

"A word, my fathers," he commanded, and in excellent Spanish.

"Go on," said Padre Flores, sternly.

"We have not come to kill," said Anastacio, slowly and

with great distinctness: the noise beyond the north gate had ceased. "You know that we never kill the priests, nor do we care for blood. We have come for the stores of the Mission - all your great winter supply, except a small quantity which we will leave you that you may not suffer until you can get more. We are tired of this life. We belong to the mountains. We cannot see that we are any better for your teachings, and we certainly are not as strong. Now let us do our work in peace, and all will be well. But if you fire, we let our arrows go, and we are twenty to one."

All turned anxiously to Padre Flores. They were not warlike, and if no bodily harm was intended they could see no reason for resistance.

"You have us at disadvantage," said Padre Flores, coldly. "I cannot sacrifice those in my charge, if you do not mean to kill. I agree to your terms on one condition: that we retain our firearms. I pass my word that no one shall shoot. I cannot take your word - nor that of any Indian. As you say, our teachings are thrown away."

"I take yours," said Anastacio, undisturbed. "All I ask is that you remain here under charge of twenty of my followers until I call them away."

He marched off, after planting his guard; and for the next two hours he and his men looted the Mission and packed the trove on horses which had been brought up, or on the backs of the bigger Indians. At the end of that time he shouted to his prisoners to come down and enter the Mission.

Roldan and Adan had been exchanging bitter

condolences over the humiliating change in the warlike programme, but the raw air of the morning had chilled their enthusiasm, and Roldan, moreover, began to feel reaction from the shock to his nerves. It was not every day that a boy sailed down through forty feet of space and lit on his feet, and his nerves were out of tune.

When Anastacio called, he went with the rest, but lagged behind. The door of the Mission sala was open. The priests entered first, their heads scornfully erect; then the brethren, the soldiers, and servants. As Roldan and Adan were about to enter, the door was suddenly pulled to, coarse hands were clapped over their mouths, and, kicking, struggling, biting, scratching, they were borne swiftly across the courtyard and out of the gates. There they were set on their feet, and found themselves face to face with Anastacio.

"Don't yell," he said. "There is no one to come to the rescue. We shall not hurt you unless you try to run away. Then I myself will beat you. Get on that horse, both of you."

"I am tired," said Roldan, indifferently. "I want to sleep."

"Sleep? Very well. Come here."

He lifted him upon a large horse, then mounted behind and encircled him with one arm.

"Go to sleep," he said; and cantered rapidly down the valley, followed by his thieving horde.

VII

When Roldan awoke he shivered slightly: the breath of winter was about him. He peered into the dusk, but could only gather that he was in a forest of huge trees on the side of a mountain. High above the wind was surging. He had a curious sense of travelling through the depths of the sea in a vacuum, the roar of suspended waters just over his head. Behind, between the giant trees, was a moving column of horses and men.

"Where are we?" he asked Anastacio.

"In the mountains, in a redwood forest. My pueblo is not far."

"What mountains? What forest?"

"That you will not know."

"Where is Adan?"

"On a stout mustang between two faithful followers of mine."

"They are unnecessary. He would not leave me."

"Perhaps not. Sometimes the white man lies and

sometimes he is true."

Roldan sat up; his tired head had rested against the shoulder of his captor.

"Suppose I get behind you," he said. "It will be more comfortable for us both. That is, if you can trust me," with an attempt at sarcasm.

"I trust you. Get behind."

Roldan slipped down, sprang up, then strained his eyes once more into the depths of the forest. Nothing moved but that winding procession. Occasionally a coyote yapped or a wildcat yelled. Suddenly something fell against his face, pricking it gently. He looked over Anastacio's shoulder. They were passing into an open. The air was full of white, whirling particles.

"It snows," said Anastacio; "but we are soon there."

"We are in the Sierras," thought Roldan. He looked about with intense interest; he had never seen snow before; and to penetrate the mystery of the mighty Sierras had been one of the hopes of his life. The ground was white, and crunched under the horses' hoofs. The air was thick with snow-stars glittering under the full radiance of the moon. Roldan forgot that he was a captive. His mind had made its first impulse to the mysteries of night and solitude during the few moments between his entry into another forest and the encounter with the bear; it now made its first real opening. He was vaguely troubled by the embryonic thoughts that in their maturity come to men who have lived and suffered, when they are alone in a forest at night, far from other men.

Again they plunged into the forest. No snow penetrated the treetops, knit together by centuries and storms. All was black again, and the deep ocean of leaf and branch roared faintly overhead.

Roldan felt oppressed and thoughtful. He looked into the future and saw himself a man. He would be governor of the Californias, and make himself a good and great man, wiser than the idle caballeros who patronised him; he would teach them the folly of their useless lives.

"Look," said Anastacio, abruptly. "We are here. It is a pueblo of my fathers, and will serve us now."

He pointed with his riding switch through the trees to a vague whiteness, and in a moment they emerged into another open. It was a clearing some three hundred feet square, crowded with dilapidated hovels, white under a light fall of snow. It was in the heart of the Sierras, on the flat of a peak; and high on every side reared other peaks, glittering with snow, black with redwoods. The snow clouds had passed. The moon rode in a dark blue sky set thick with stars. The silence, the repose, were appalling.

Roldan jumped to the ground, and accompanied by Anastacio, ran up and down to get the cold and fatigue of night travel out of his body. In a few moments they were joined by Adan, who came waddling up, his broad face knit with perplexity and delight.

"I leave you now," said Anastacio, "but remember - if you attempt to escape you carry poisoned arrows in your backs."

"Ay, Roldan!" exclaimed Adan, when their formidable host was out of hearing. "But this was more than we bargained for. I don't know whether I like it or not."

"I must say I don't like the idea of being in the power of savages - Indians," said Roldan, contemptuously. "But as we started out for adventure we must take black bread with white. I think I do rather like this, but I shall not if we have to stay here too long and nothing happens."

"Isn't anything likely to happen?" asked Adan, anxiously.

"How can one tell? And who could find this place? But if worst comes to worst we'll run away - and not with poisoned arrows in our backs, either."

"That we will," said Adan, emphatically. "We've done that before."

The boys were given a good supper of meat roasted over coals, and a slice of Mission cake, then were escorted by Anastacio to the largest of the huts.

"Enter and sleep," he said. "It is my hut. I shall sleep beside you."

VIII

The boys slept soundly between two excellent Mission blankets in a corner of the hut, whose walls and floors had been well swept with Mission brooms. Anastacio, despite his contempt for the trammels of civilisation, had developed an aristocratic taste or two. He slept by the door, but when the boys awoke he was not there. The pueblo, but for two sentinels standing before the door, was apparently deserted. The sun was looking over the highest peak, suffusing the black aisles of the forest with a rosy glow, reddening the snow on hut and level and rocky heights. There was not a sound except the faint murmur of the treetops.

"Where is the world?" asked Roldan. "Are there ranches, with cavalcades and bull-fights, lazy caballeros lying in hammocks smoking cigarritos, or dancing the night through with silly girls? Dios de mi alma! I feel as if I did not care."

"Caramba!" exclaimed Adan, "I am famished. Do you suppose they have left us anything to eat?"

"I suppose there is nothing to do but ask one of these dogs to be good enough to give us breakfast - no, not ask. I could starve, but not beg of an Indian."

He beckoned haughtily to one of the sentinels, who

Gertrude Atherton

approached and saluted respectfully.

"Breakfast," said the young don, curtly. "We wish to eat at once."

The Indian went over to a large stone oven and took out four meal cakes, which he carried to the boys, then fetched them fruit and wine.

"Where is Anastacio and the others?" asked Roldan, breakfast over.

"In the temascal."

Roldan sprang to his feet. "Do you hear that, Adan?" he cried. "We have always wanted to see Indians in temascal." To the sentinel, "Take us there at once."

The Indian scowled. "But for you, senor, we, too, are in the temascal."

"Take us to the temascal," said Roldan, peremptorily, and the savage, in whom servility had been planted by civilisation, yielded to the will of the aristocrat. He bent his shoulders and said: "Bueno; come!"

The boys followed him through the brush, the sweet-scented chaparral on which the honey-dew still lingered, to another and smaller clearing. Here were several long rows of earthen huts, three or four feet high, out of which smoke poured through an aperture in the roof of each. Near by was a broad creek to which the bank sloped gently from the clearing. The creek, some three feet deep, murmured over coloured stones and sprouting trees. The long fine strands of the ice grass trailed far over the water, motionless. Huge bunches of maidenhair, delicate as green lace, clung to the steep bluffs on the opposite side. Forests of ferns grew close to the water's edge. Down through a rift in the cliffs tumbled a mountain stream over its rocky bed.

"Are they stewing in those things?" asked Roldan.

The Indian nodded. Roldan, followed closely by Adan, approached one of the temascals and opened the door cautiously. At first they could see nothing, so dense was the smoke; but when much had rushed out through the new opening, they saw two prostrate figures, sweating from every pore. Their eyes were closed, they breathed stertorously. The expression on their heavy faces was beatific.

"Caramba!" exclaimed Adan, as Roldan closed the door, "I am glad they like it. What a lot of trouble to get clean."

"As they never take a bath, they couldn't get clean any other way; and besides it rests them after any great exertion - Mission raiding, for instance - and they also fancy it drags every humour out through the pores of the skin. They'll be coming out soon. Let us go down to the creek and wait."

The smoke was ascending upward in straight columns through the still air, scarcely clouding the brilliant morning, not a wreath wandering into the aisles of the forest. The sun climbed higher, melting the light fall of snow, its rays dancing among the silver ripples of the water, vivifying the many greens about the creek.

The boys amused themselves flinging pebbles at the

darting trout and discussing chances of escape.

"We must not fly too soon," said Roldan, "or we shall run into the soldiers. Of course they are scouring the country after these robbers."

"This is a good place to hide in until the Mission food gives out; but I'd prefer even the barracks to living on acorns - Ay, look!"

The door of one of the temascals had opened. A limp figure tottered forth and down to the bank. He almost fell into the creek, but had sufficient wit uncooked to rest his head on a projecting stone. Presently came another, then another, and another, until the bright rocks were covered with dusky forms, the heads bobbing just above the surface, supported on stump or stone. The boys barely recognised Anastacio. Where was that commanding presence, that haughty mien? Bowed like an old man, blind from smoke, with simmering brain, he reeled into the water with as little dignity as his creatures.

But in less than an hour all had sprung forth briskly, danced about in the sun to dry, and started on a run for the pueblo. Roldan and Adan followed close, knowing that a feast alone would satisfy appetite after the temascal. And in a little time the smell of roast meat pervaded the morning, great cakes were roasting. The boys were invited to eat apart with Anastacio. At the conclusion of the meal the host, who had not spoken, solemnly poured out three glasses of fire-water. He swallowed his at a gulp. The boys sipped a few drops, winking rapidly. Then Roldan thought it time to speak: his chief was visibly thawed.

"What are you keeping us for?" he asked.

"Ransom." Anastacio lit a cigarrito - one of the padre's - and lay back on a bearskin.

"Do you know why we ran away? To escape the conscription. If you give us up, all our adventures, our dangers, our escapes, will be as nothing, and we shall be punished besides."

Anastacio moved his eyes to Roldan's with a flash of interest.

"Good! I hate the government. You shall stay here until the time of conscription is over. Then I will get a big sack of Mexican dollars, a herd of cattle, a caponara of horses, and much tobacco and whiskey. Who are your fathers?"

Roldan explained.

Anastacio flushed under his thick skin. "Good. I will double the ransom - and the guard."

"The conscription will be over in a few weeks -"

"You could not go before. We too must hide. Of course the soldiers are behind. I have many scouts watching. Now go to sleep."

The following week was clear and bright, but very cold. The boys, bred in the warm basin of California, must have suffered had not Anastacio ordered one of his minions to make them coat and boots from the skin of the coyote. Every morning the chief drilled his men with the tactics of a born commander who had let no opportunity for observation escape him. The military discipline of the pueblo was only relaxed for three hours in the afternoon, during which time the Indians were given full taste of the freedom they coveted that they might battle for it the more passionately when the time came. They gambled, slept, shot game in the forest, exercised the horses, which were in corral about a mile from the camp. The boys shot deer with Anastacio, and wrestled in the plaza. Occasionally the taciturn Indian unbent when sitting by the great bonfire in the open at night, and told wild tales of savage life before the padres came. Roldan admired his splendid supple body and fearless manhood, but the Indian was too sinister to inspire affection. Adan was loudly bored. Roldan's ardent imagination sustained him.

At the end of the week the scouts having failed to discover any sign of the enemy, Anastacio determined to go down to the river in the valley for a fortnight's salmon fishing. He, too, was bored. The fangs of civilisation are long and tenacious.

It was on a brilliant winter's morning that Anastacio, his captives, and his five hundred men wound their way down through the cold forest on the mountain into the soft warm air of the valley. There had been no rain for three weeks, and the river was not more than half full; and it was very quiet. They camped on the bank, well away from the scattered groups of trees, that they might not lose a ray of sunshine; and Roldan and Adan forgot that they were under constant surveillance. There were no tents; they slept in the open air, the boys in the centre of a square of Indians. During the day they caught many fine salmon, and salted what they did not eat, to sell to the rancheros.

It was on the sixth night that Roldan, who was wakeful, suddenly raised himself on his elbow and listened intently. Far away, above the murmur of the river, the audible slumbers of the camp, he heard a low, precise, monotonous sound. He knew what it meant. For a moment he hesitated. The chances of escape seemed to grow less daily. It was true that he was in no danger, that he would eventually be restored to his parents - but with his adventures cut short. He was fond of his home, but it was always there, and he was keen for variety: his life had been very uneventful. On the other hand, if that advancing army conquered the Indians, might not his and Adan's captivity be far more distasteful than it was at present? He sprang up and called Anastacio. In a second that warrior was on his feet and had leaped over his alert sentinels into the square.

"What is it?" he demanded.

"Listen."

Anastacio threw himself full length and laid his ear to the ground. A moment later he was erect again. He caught Roldan by one shoulder and Adan by the other. By this time every Indian in the camp was pressing about his chief.

"They are not two miles away," said Anastacio. "And the dawn will be here in an hour. There are ten miles between us and the mountains. I don't wish to fight in the open without knowing their numbers."

Roldan danced up and down with sudden excitement. "I have a plan," he cried. "You can trust me. I don't want to go back."

Anastacio bent his keen malevolent eyes close above the young Spaniard's, then loosened his hold.

"Bueno," he said. "I trust you."

"The straw," said Roldan. "Bring it all here."

Anastacio gave the order, and an immense carreta of straw was trundled up.

"Now," said Roldan, "gather it into bunches the size of a man's head and tie each firmly. The tide is running toward the enemy, and it is too dark to see clearly. Do you understand, senor?"

Anastacio made a loud exclamation, caught Roldan in his arms and kissed. him, much to that haughty young gentleman's disgust, then tied the first bunch himself. Roldan, Adan, and some forty of the quicker Indians rapidly manipulated the straw, and in little more than ten minutes had cast a hundred round compact bundles into the hurrying tide. As they sailed away they certainly looked, under the heavy shadow of the banks and the black-blue of the sky, like an army of men swimming with the desperate haste of terror, their heads alone above water.

"Now!" cried Anastacio, "to the mountains."

They had brought only pack-horses. There was nothing to do but run, and Anastacio, driving his entire following ahead of him, sped to cover. It was not twenty minutes before they heard a sharp volley of musketry, and if their breath had not been short they would have laughed aloud at the success of Roldan's strategy. The sky was turning grey as they reached the straggling outposts of the forest on the mountain. The firing had ceased. Their ruse had doubtless been discovered.

"We will hide for twenty-four hours and rest," Anastacio said to Roldan, who was the only person he condescended to hold converse with, although he allowed Adan to sun himself in his presence. "By that time, too, I shall know their numbers. If they are many I'll draw them into the mountains and fire from ambush. If few, they shall have open fight."

"You will let us see it?" asked Roldan, eagerly. "Of course I cannot fight my own people; but I don't want to be sent to the pueblo, and I do want to see a fight."

Anastacio hesitated. "Bueno," he said, "I owe you much. You give me the word of the California don that unless I am killed you will not run away?"

"I promise. There is nothing else to do. That is to say, I promise not to run away before this battle is over."

"That is what I mean," said Anastacio, curtly. "Now we will sleep."

He disposed his men in the forest above a narrow, rocky canon into which the enemy would hardly venture. Roldan volunteered to keep watch with the two sentinels, and returned with them to the outskirts of the forest. The enemy was marching steadily across the valley. After a time they halted, and lay down for a time. Early in the afternoon they resumed march, then halted again within a mile of the mountain, sending two scouts ahead. By this time Anastacio had joined his sentinels, and all four hid in the underforest between the great trees.

The scouts, keeping as much under cover as was possible, crept up the lower spur of the mountain, their glance describing a constant half-circle. When they were within a few feet of the fugitives, Anastacio raised his bow and discharged two arrows in rapid succession. One buried itself in the jugular of the foremost scout, and he huddled down among the soft leaves without a cry. The other, equally well aimed, entered the shoulder of the second scout, where it quivered violently for a few seconds, then was torn forth and flung to the ground with a cry of defiance. The Californian, disregarding his wound, raised himself to his full height and pointed his pistol. But vaguely: the quiet, feathery young redwoods told no tales. Then his eye fell upon his dead brother. He turned and fled.

"They will not enter the forest," said Anastacio; "and when I am ready they will fight, not before. Have you pencil and paper, senor?"

Roldan produced a treasured note-book that a relative had brought him from Boston.

"Write," said the chief; and he dictated: -

SENOR DON CAPITAN, - At noon to-morrow we fight in the valley near the eight oak trees and the two madronos. Do you wish to fight sooner you can come into the mountains. It will be better for us.

ANASTACIO.

He tore out the leaf, crawled down the mountain as

non-apparently as a python, and pinned it high on an outstanding redwood, then returned and told his sentinels to sleep, replacing them with others.

Gertrude Atherton

IX

That evening Anastacio called Roldan to him.

"I fear treachery," he said. "Who can trust five hundred men that have learned too much? And the white men, they have better brains than mine. I watch to-night. Will you watch with me, senor? - that I can sleep before morning and rest for the fight."

"I will," said Roldan, enthusiastically. "And Adan also?"

"It matters not."

When the dusk was so thick in the aisles that every moving frond looked like a man looming suddenly, one of the sentinels returned with the news that the paper had been taken from the tree, and that the Californians had pitched tents, and to all appearance were at rest for the night.

It was not likely that the enemy would venture into the forest at night. They were not a large body, they were not pressed for time, nor were they the heroes of many wars. The Indians were comparatively safe until morning; nevertheless, Anastacio was too good a general to relax vigilance. When night came he and the two boys went down the mountain and sent the outpost back to sleep. They ventured out where the trees grew far apart, and the brilliant stars of California illumined the great valley like so many thousand watch-fires.

The three sat down side by side, their gaze directed steadily downward and outward.

"Why do you fight at all?" asked Roldan. "You could stay in these mountains until the Californians were dust, and not be caught."

"And live like hunted beasts. I like the valley; the sun in winter, the cool mountains in summer. If I am victor to-morrow, all the Indians in California will call me chief. They will run here from every Mission and hacienda, and from every hill and mountain, like little ones to their good father; and we will drive the priests out of the country, and make the hidalgos, the caballeros, the soft silk-dressed donas our friends or our slaves - as they wish. California belongs to us. The Great Spirit put us here, not the white man. If it was for them why did they not grow out of the earth as we did? Why were we put here at all if our land was not for us? We were happy until these priests came to drive us mad making boots and mud bricks and wine all day, driven like dogs to the kennel, flogged when we wanted to lie in the sun -"

"But, Anastacio," interrupted Roldan, who had listened to this strange outburst with the vague consciousness that the soul of an expiring race had opened its lips for a brief moment, "you are far more clever than most Indians. If it were not for the priests you would be no better than the most ignorant of them."

"If I am clever now, senor, was I not clever in the

Gertrude Atherton

beginning? You do not make cake out of bran. The Great Spirit sent his light into me and said: 'Thou shalt be a great chief.' I could have done as well and better without the priests. What good did it do me to read and tell my beads and make chocolate? Was I happy at the Mission? Not for one moon, senor. I felt as if I had a wild beast chained in me that choked and panted for the free life of my youth, of my fathers. I ran away from the Mission twenty-three times - and was brought back and flogged. Many times I would have crushed my head with a stone had it not been that all the other Indians of the Mission ran to me like dogs, and that I could make them tremble with a word and obey with a look. I knew that the Great Spirit had given me what these poor creatures had not, and that one day I would give California to them again. It has begun."

"But we have better things to eat and drink and more comfortable houses and clothes than you have in your pueblos. I like what the priests call 'civilisation.'"

"It is for the white man, not for the Indian with a skin like the earth and a heart like the wild-cat. If we did not know of fine bread and thin wine and heavy shoes and cursed bags about our legs we should not want them. Padre Flores says that he and the other priests came here to make us happy. Why not let us be happy in our own way? We needed no teaching."

Years after, Roldan, who grew to know the world well and many men, recalled the conversation of that night, and meditated upon the strange workings of the human mind: the fundamental philosophy of life differs little in the brain of the savage and the brain of the student-thinker.

"We are told that we must progress, grow better," he said.

"Hundreds and hundreds of years Indians lived and died here before the priests came. All legends say they were happy. Now they 'progress,' and suffer - in the body and in the spirit. One life is for us, another for you. Should the white man have many children and children's children until all the mountains and valleys of California are his, then will all the Indians die, even though they are treated well for they are slaves - no more. Are they happy? For what were they made? To be slaves and die from the earth before they are threescore and ten, to be no more remembered than the beasts of the field?"

"I hope you'll win to-morrow," cried Roldan, his young mind moved to pity, and profoundly disturbed. "You can never get California away from the Spaniard, and I can't wish you to; but you might, if you rallied all the Indians to you, become powerful enough to live in the way you like, best, and I hope you will. Why should men say: 'I am better than you; I will make you like myself?' How do we know? I have ridden like the wind, and coliared a bull with the best vaquero in the Californias, but I am afraid my mind has had fifteen years of siesta. Now - well, I shall be governor of the Californias one day, and then I shall send all the Indians back to the mountains."

Anastacio put out his hand, and the two civilisations decreed by Nature to stand apart from the beginning to the end of time clasped in brief friendship.

"I will be your friend," said the Indian, "and the white man need not despise the friendship of a great chief.

California is a fair land. Others will come to it besides the Spaniard. If Anastacio has thousands of Indians to run to his call they will fight when he bids them."

"Caramba! you are right," exclaimed Roldan. "Those Americans -"

"American boys?" asked Adan, eagerly.

"Now," said Anastacio, "I sleep. Awake me when the sky turns grey."

He stretched himself out and slept at once. The boys drew close together and speculated upon the fateful morrow. They agreed to remain close together, out of sight of the enemy, but where they could watch the Indian forces. If Anastacio fell they would flee at once.

X

The small Californian force - it numbered little over two hundred men - was under the command of Juan Pardo Mesa, a captain notable for his victorious encounters with Indians and for his knowledge of their cunning. He was on the alert at dawn next morning, and long before the sun had spurned the tops of the Coast range, his assumption of meditated treachery was confirmed. A rising wind had set the young redwoods in motion. Before long the practised eye of Captain Mesa saw an increased agitation among the feathery branches, his ear caught a slight crackling. His men were flat on the ground. He stood in the shadow of a large oak. A moment later a dusky form crept out to where the brush grew more sparsely, hesitated a moment, and apparently passed back word that all was well; he was immediately followed by many of his kind; and the lower slope of the mountain, burnt bare by fire, seemed suddenly swarming with huge black rats.

Mesa waited until they were well away from cover, then gave the expected order: two hundred muskets, carbines, and flintlock pistols were discharged, and one piece of artillery.

But Anastacio, no mean general himself, was also on the alert for the unexpected. In a few moments he had

Gertrude Atherton

marshalled his forces in the form of a hollow square, and ordered them to discharge their arrows from a recumbent position. Owing to the heavy shadows, the aim of the Californians had been uncertain, and only a few of the Indians had fallen. Roldan and Adan were safe behind two large redwoods just above the Indian army.

The firing continued steadily all the morning, but resulted in few mortal wounds. There was not a poisoned arrow in the pueblo. The balls did more serious damage, and several Indians rolled groaning down the slope. The rest were undaunted. They were more than two to one, and had implicit faith in their chief's assurance that they were bound to rout the Spaniard.

Under cover of the cloud of smoke his weapons had raised despite a strong wind, Mesa executed two flank movements, justifying the tactics of Anastacio: he detached forty men from the main body and directed them to attack the Indians on both sides and to cut off their retreat to the forest. They were almost upon the north and south ends of Anastacio's square - after making a detour and advancing from a distance - when the boys shouted a warning. In a moment arrows were flying to right and left; and the answering volley was far more deadly than the effects of firing up hill. The Indians stood their ground, fitting their arrows with swift dexterity, encouraged by Anastacio, who glided from point to point like a hungry cobra, discharging two arrows to every man's one. His only hope was to keep the Californians at long range until losses compelled the latter to retreat: at close quarters arrows would be no match for firearms.

The battle began at five in the morning. It was at four in the afternoon that Roldan passed his hand across his burning eyeballs, then gripped Adan's arm and said through his teeth, -

"Anastacio is hit. I saw him shake from head to foot."

"Madre de dios! Shall we run?"

"Not yet. My brain is on fire. War is awful, and yet I burn to have a pistol in my hands. I am sorry for Anastacio - but Dios de mi alma! - to see a brave Spanish officer bite the dust with the arrow of a dog in his brain! Ay, he moves! He is not dead."

"His hand is as steady - but - do you notice? - all are not firing."

"The arrows are giving out. There is only one end. But I must see it through. Mary! Mary! They are breaking."

The Indians, finding themselves almost without arrows, had sprung to their feet, intending to make a rush for cover; but Mesa had anticipated this move, and almost immediately his men had closed with the savages, knocking them on the head with the butt-end of their muskets, discharging their pistols at short range. The Indians. used both tooth and nail, yelling like wildcats. The cool imperturbability of the earlier part of the day had fled with their arrows. Anastacio fought like a tiger. Despite his wounded thigh he stood firmly on his feet, snatched the musket from a man his hands had throttled, and whirled it about his head, threatening death to all that approached. His face was swollen with passion, his eyes were starting from their sockets, his long hair tossed wildly. The boys watched him with cold extremities and hot cheeks and eyes. They were oblivious to the rest of the battlefield. The fate of the indomitable chief, upon whose life the freedom of a race perhaps depended, would have riveted the attention of older and wiser brains. His movements were easy to follow: he was head above all and shoulders above many.

Suddenly the boys gave a gasp. The head of Anastacio was no longer to be seen above that surging throng. Had he been wounded in a vital part? A moment later they gave a hoarse gurgling cry and clung together, shaking like children in icy water. The head of Anastacio rose again - above the crowd, then higher, - higher, - until it looked down upon the squirming mass from six feet above. It was on the end of a pole.

XI

The boys turned and fled, scrambling blindly upwards. Instinctively they ran in the direction of the pueblo, and when they were finally obliged to sit down and fight for their lost breath they realised the course they had taken.

The horror was still in their eyes, but neither spoke of what for a long while to come must be uppermost in his mind.

"I think we may as well go to the pueblo," said Roldan, as soon as he could speak. "We must have food, and we are very tired. We can rest there a few days, then take two of the horses - we can do nothing without horses - and start out again. If any of the Indians escape and come back, they will not have spirit enough left to touch us."

"Bueno," said Adan. "The Mission blankets are there and they are soft, and that oven makes good cakes. I hope the Indians go all with the soldiers. I never want to see another."

The boys resumed their flight, but more leisurely. They had no difficulty in keeping to the trail, but it wound over many a weary mile.

Gertrude Atherton

Night comes early in the mountain forest, and before two hours had passed they were groping their way along the narrow road cut through the dense brush, and clinging to each other. They were brave lads; but long fasting, and excitement, and a terrible climax to the most trying day of their lives, had flung gunpowder among their nerves.

It was midnight when they reached the pueblo. The stars illumined fitfully the deserted huts, black in the heavy shadows. A coyote was yapping dismally, owls hooted in the forest. Both boys had a vision of deep beds and hot suppers on the ranchos of their respective parents, but they shut their teeth and raided the larder. There they found well-cured meats and dried fruits, which appeased their mighty appetites; then they went into Anastacio's hut, and wrapping themselves in the Mission blankets were soon asleep.

It was Adan who awoke Roldan violently in the morning.

"The soldiers!" he whispered hoarsely.

Roldan, rubbing the sleep from his eyes, peered through a rift between the wall of the hut and the shrunken hide which formed the door. A half dozen soldiers stood in the plaza, glancing speculatively about.

"I see no trace of them," said one. 'I cannot believe they would come back to this place. Surely it was, as I said, more natural for them to hide at the edge of the forest until we had gone."

"That dog said there was food here, and that they were

more afraid of us than of a long walk at night. Wherever they are, we find them. They are a prize second only to the head of Anastacio. Search the huts."

Roldan sprang to his feet, pulling Adan with him. "Come," he said; "follow me, and run as if you were as lean as a coyote. Remember they won't shoot."

He flung aside the hide door. The two boys flashed out and round the corner of the hut before the tired eyes and brains of the soldiers had time to grasp the happening. A moment later they were in hot pursuit, firing in the air, shouting terrific threats. But the rested and agile legs of the boys had a good start, and plunged into narrow ways where horses could not follow; and doubling, twisting, following paths but recently beaten by Anastacio in pursuit of deer, Roldan and Adan were soon far beyond the reach or ken of the men of war. It was an hour, however, before they thought it wise to arrest their flight and pause to recuperate in a redwood tree hollowed by fire. Two weeks of exposure and unwonted exertions had hardened Adan's superfluous flesh, and he was scarcely more spent than his clean-limbed friend, although every step had been taken with protest.

"Caramba!" he said, in a hoarse whisper at length. "When I am back on the rancho I won't walk for a year."

"You will have the habit by that time, my friend, and will walk in your sleep. When I am governor you will be generalissimo of all the forces and will keep your army as lively as an ant-hill."

"That is too long ahead, and we have not enough wind

Gertrude Atherton

to argue about it. What are we going to do now? How shall we get horses to leave this forest? Where shall we sleep to-night? What shall we have for dinner? I could eat a whole side of venison."

"Well, you won't, my friend. Let me think."

After a time he said: "We must stay here until night. Then we will go back to the pueblo if we can find the way. As for food, we can have none to-day. There are no berries at this time of year, and we have nothing to shoot game with. Other people have gone the day without food, and we can. When we get back to the pueblo, even if we cannot reach the larder, we can find the corral without being seen. I don't believe that the soldiers have found it, and the Indians in charge of the mustangs will let us have two when they know what has happened. Now, do not let us talk. It will make us more hungry."

Adan groaned, but accepted the decree of silence. The day wore on to noon, and in the unbroken stillness the boys ventured out of the grimy tree and lay at full length on the turf. The great redwoods towered in endless corridors, their straight columns unbroken by branch or twig for a hundred and fifty feet. Through the green close arbours above came an occasional rift of sunshine, but the aisles were full of cold green light. The boys shivered in their coyote skin coats and drew close together; they dared not run about to keep warm; they must husband their strength, and hunger was biting. There was no wind in the tree-tops, no murmur of creek, only the low hum of the forest, that in their strained ear-sense grew to a roar. Finally they fell asleep, and it was dark when Roldan awoke. He shook Adan.

"Come," he said; and his partner, grumbling but acquiescent, got to his feet and tramped heavily over the soft ground.

They had fled beyond paths, and Roldan could only trust to his locality sense, which he knew to be good. But more than once they were brought to halt before a wall of brush, which no man could have penetrated without an axe. Then they would feel their way along its irregular bristling side for a mile or more before it thinned sufficiently for egress. Frequently they heard the deadly rattle, and more than once the near cry of a panther, but there was nothing to do but push on. Precautions would have availed them nothing, and there was no refuge nearer than the pueblo. Sometimes they walked down aisles unchoked by brush but full of moving shadows, above which sounded the lonely continuous hooting of the owl. Now and again bats whirred past, and once a startled wildcat scurried across the path and darted up a tree, crying with terror.

"If we only don't meet a bear," thought Roldan, who dared not speak lest his voice should shake courage and terrors apart.

It was midnight when Adan announced with what emphasis was left in him, -

"We are lost."

Roldan answered through his teeth: "Yes, but I think I hear the creek. When we find that, all we have to do is to follow it south."

"My heart is in the South," muttered Adan. "We might follow that."

Gertrude Atherton

"I am ashamed of you," said Roldan, with a lofty scorn which was good for five words and no more.

It was a half hour later that they stood upon the high bank of the creek and looked gratefully up at the broad strip of night light. After the dense shadows of the forest the cold light of stars seemed more radiant than noon-day.

"We cannot follow along the bank for more than a little way at a time, on account of the ferns and brush," said Roldan. "We should walk three times the distance, and perhaps get lost again. I am going to wade. Will you?"

"Madre de dios! And get rheumatism? My teeth clack together at the thought."

"You will not be able to keep still long enough to get rheumatism, my friend. By the grace of Mary we shall be on horseback all day to-morrow. The water is not a foot deep, and the chill only lasts a moment. Take off your boots."

"What is left of them," muttered Adan. But they were better than no boots, and he took them off, and slung them round his neck. Roldan scrambled down the bank and plunged into the creek. Adan, after a moment's hesitation, followed with audible reluctance. He thrust the tip of one foot into the icy water, withdrew it with a shout, tried the other; then seeing that Roldan was splashing far ahead, jumped in with both feet and ran along the slippery rocks, wondering when the change of temperature would occur. His teeth clattered loudly. He pulled in and executed a war-dance on the stones, then sat down on a fallen boulder and rubbed his feet violently. Roldan kept steadily on, mindful of his dignity as leader; but only as Adan joined him had his teeth ceased from clattering and the warmth crawled back to his feet.

Cold, hungry, inexpressibly weary, the boys plodded on, sometimes in the clear light of stars, sometimes under the chill blackness of meeting trees. Fish and other slimy things darted across their feet; they stepped to their waists into more than one treacherous pool. The dark blue of the sky had turned to grey when Roldan raised his arm and pointed to a squat dark object on the summit of the cliff.

"A hut," he said. "We are at the pueblo."

The boys crawled softly up the almost perpendicular bank and peered over the edge. To all appearances the pueblo was deserted. If the soldiers were there - and their horses were not - they slept within the huts. The animal instinct, so bravely repressed, overcame the adventurers. They ran across the open to the hut where the food was kept, and ate for fifteen minutes without speaking or taking the trouble to hide themselves.

Gertrude Atherton

XII

When they had satisfied their appetites they made two large packages of dried meat and fruit, tying them securely with straw to their right arms: saddle-bags there were none.

"Not a horse," whispered Adan. "Do you think the soldiers have gone?"

"I think they are lost, and as they did not stop to tie their horses when they started after us, they won't see them again until they get back to camp. Come."

Roldan peered cautiously into each of the huts in turn; all were empty. Then the boys started for the corral, which the soldiers would not have passed either on their way to the pueblo or in pursuit of the runaways. They found the Indians in charge sound asleep in their hut, and did not think it worth while to awaken them. The two mustangs they led forth, vicious brutes at best, were very restless from prolonged inactivity. Roldan's submitted to the saddle, but bolted as soon as he felt a determined pair of legs about his sides; and as our adventurer had neither whip nor spurs, all he could do was to hang on and shout to Adan to follow close. This was the only thing that Adan's mustang was willing to do, and the boys were borne blindly on, down one path, up another, plunging deeper into the black recesses of the forest until they knew no more of their whereabouts than if they had dropped from another sphere.

After many weary miles the mustangs slackened, and the boys dismounted and cut two slender but stinging whips. After that they rose once more to the proud supremacy of man over brute. But the situation was full of peril. They were hopelessly lost, the redwoods were the home of the grizzly and the panther, and they might come upon the soldiers at any moment. But there was nothing to do but to ride on, and at least they had horses and food.

They descended whenever descent was possible, for at the foot of the mountain lay the open valley; but there were no trails; in all likelihood they were where no man, red or white, had ever been before; they had to force their way where the brush was thinnest, and as often their flight was toward loftier heights.

As the day wore on the temperature fell, even in those forest depths where the sun had not penetrated for a thousand years. The beauty of the forest palled upon Roldan: those everlasting aisles with their grey motionless columns, their green sinister light, the delicate fern wood below, the dense mat of branch and leaf so high above. The redwoods oppress and terrify when they have man completely at their mercy. They look as if they could speak if they would, roar louder than the storms that have never shaken them. But they know the value of silence, and the silence of their inmost depths is awful.

After many hours the boys rode out upon a bare peak. But its outlook told them nothing. Behind rose other

Gertrude Atherton

peaks, below was the dense primeval forest, rising and falling on other slopes. There was no glimpse of valley anywhere. The sky was heavy with the grey lurid clouds of concentrated storm.

"We will eat," said Roldan, briefly: "but not too much."

They tethered the mustangs that the beasts might eat of the abundant grass, and consumed a small quantity of their store. Then they stretched at full length on the ground to rest their weary bodies.

"Let us stay here the night," said Adan, with a cavernous yawn.

"It is hardly darker by night than by day in the forest, but perhaps it is well to rest."

"I am one ache, no more," murmured Adan, and went to sleep.

Roldan pillowed his head on his arm and for once followed lead. He awoke suddenly, his face wet and stinging. White stars were whirling, the ground was white, the forest was half obliterated.

He shook Adan and dragged him to his feet.

"We must get into the redwoods at once," he said. "We shall be buried here."

Adan gasped but cinched his saddle; the boys sprang upon the now tractable mustangs and plunged into the forest below. The brush was thin, and they pushed their way downward as rapidly as the steep descent would permit. Sometimes the forest protected them from the storm, at others the trees grew wide apart and the riders were exposed to its pitiless rush. In these open spaces they could see nothing, could only push blindly on, brushing the stinging particles from their faces, their hands and feet almost numb. The snow in the open was already as high as the horses' knees. There was no wind, only that silent sweeping of the heavens. In the depths the high branches of the redwoods groaned ominously under the stiffening weight, like giants in pain.

The forest thinned. The snow had its will of the earth. There was no refuge under the larger trees that still stood, like outposts, here and there; the branches were too high above. Once Adan suggested through his stiff lips and unruly teeth that they turn back and take refuge in some dense grove above; but Roldan shook his head peremptorily. He had heard of the fearful storms of the Sierras; they lasted for days, and the snow stood its ground for weeks. Their only hope was the valley.

But they descended only to rise again: in the white darkness of the storm they dared not attempt to skirt the base of the peaks; they must keep straight on, to the west, for there lay the valley.

Occasionally, where a grove of trees stood close and the snow lay shallow, the boys got off and wrestled, rousing the blood in their legs and arms; then urged their mustangs to greater speed. But the poor brutes were very weary, and the blood in their veins was almost torpid. Once they stood still and shook, whinnying pitifully. A huge grizzly, so powdered as to be hardly distinguishable from the drifts about him, floundered along to the right. The boys crossed themselves and awaited their fate, with the apathy of numb and despairing brains; but the monster was evidently aiming for the warmth of his home, and took no notice of the meal in four courses standing in the middle of the path.

The night deepened. The snow thickened and sped down with an audible rush, a sting in each beautiful white bee. The boys nodded, roused themselves, fell forward, their arms mechanically stiffening about the horses' necks. Once they flung out their hands and feet with a smothered shriek. A tongue of flame seemed to leap down their throats and hiss through their veins, while the world roared and heaved about them. Then all sensation was over.

XIII

Roldan opened his eyes. His brain was heavy; he was conscious only of an intense warmth. His arms appeared to be bound to his sides, his whole body in a vise. He kicked out with a vigorous return of the instinct of independence. The action shook his brain free and he understood: he was tightly wrapped in a blanket, and there were other blankets upon him. He raised his head. The room was one of familiar lineaments, - whitewashed walls, a mat by the iron bed, an altar in the corner, linen with elaborate drawn-work on bureau and washstand. The blood poured upward to the young adventurer's face. Was this his room? Had he been ill and dreamed strange happenings? He freed his arms and sat up. No; there was no room in his father's house exactly like this, monotonous as were the furnishing and architecture of the time.

He took his head between his hands and thought; the events of the past weeks marched through his brain in rapid and precise succession - up to a certain point: his senses had been frozen in the Sierras. From a raging snowstorm to this blistering bed all was blank.

He disencumbered himself, slipped to the floor, and opened the door, then scrambled back to bed as best he could; his legs felt as if they had been boned. He was

Gertrude Atherton

also one vast desire for food and drink. But that glimpse through the door had raised his spirits. He was in a great adobe house surrounding a court in which a fountain splashed among ferns and little orange-trees. It was the house of a grandee, but there was none like it in the neighbourhood of the Rancho de los Palos Verdes.

He waited with what patience he could muster until his open door should attract attention, listening to the murmur of the fountain, inhaling the fragrance of orange and magnolia, wondering if Adan, too, were safe, angrily resenting his weakness.

The door cautiously opened wide, and a woman, stout, brown, but of exceeding grace and elegance, entered and bent over him.

"Good-day, senora," said Roldan, politely. "I am very hungry. Where am I? And is Adan here?"

The lady smiled and patted his cheek with a shapely and flashing hand.

"He is well and sleeping, my son, and you are both in the Casa of Don Tiburcio Carillo, of the Rancho Encarnarcion, in a great valley many, many leagues from the Sierras and the snow - Madre de dios! Pobrecitos! So cold you must have been, so frightened - and you the sons of great rancheros, no?"

Roldan modestly named his fortunate status, then sat up and kissed her hand, as he had seen his gallant brothers kiss the hands of lovely young donas. The lady looked much pleased and drew a chair beside the bed. Roldan wondered if he should ever satisfy his raging appetite, but was too polite to mention the subject again, and determined to satisfy his curiosity instead.

"Senora, tell me how we came here," he asked. "My head will burst until I know."

"Our bell mare, the most valuable on our rancho, strayed far the day before yesterday. All that day and the next six vaqueros looked for her. One traced her to the Sierras and went on in spite of the storm. He found her, and, just afterward - you. He thought you were dead, but poured aguardiente down your throats. You swallowed but did not awaken, although he shook you and pounded you. Then he strapped your friend - Adan, no? upon the back of Lolita, took you in his arms, and galloped for home - you were almost at the foot of the mountain. Ay! but I was frightened when you came. Gracias a dios that you are well and not frozen. Bueno, I go to send you a good breakfast. Hasta luego."

She went out, and Roldan lay wondering if the breakfast were already cooked. The door opened again. Roldan sat up. But it was Adan. He wore a long nightgown and dug his knuckles into his eyes. His knees, too, were shaky.

"Hist, Roldan," he whispered loudly. "Are you there, or do I dream?"

"Come into my bed and have breakfast - breakfast, Adan!"

Adan gathered his remaining energies, bolted across the room, and climbed into bed.

"Dios de mi alma, Roldan," he gasped. "Where are we, and why are we sweltered like sick babies? This is a fine place. Ay! may I never see snow nor a redwood again!"

Roldan told what he knew of the beginning of their new chapter, and soon after he finished two Indian servants entered with trays, set them on the bed, and retired.

"Ay! this looks like home," cried Adan, almost in tears. "Chocolate! Tortillas! Chicken with yellow rice!" He crossed himself fervently and attacked the fragrant meal.

It was not a large breakfast, for it was many hours since they had eaten before; they left not a grain of rice nor a shred on a bone. But half-satisfied, although very comfortable, they made up their minds to dress. On the chair was a complete outfit, suitable for a young don. Roldan concluded it had been thoughtfully placed at his disposal that he might not appear in the sala of Casa Carillo garbed like a coyote. How he hated the memory of that ugly and infested garment.

"I, too, have a silk jacket and breeches by my bed," said Adan, "and a lace shirt and silk stockings, and shoes with buckles. There must be those of our age in the Casa Carillo, my friend. Bueno! I go to make a caballero of myself. Hasta luego."

He opened the door and peered out, then ran hastily down the corridor to his room. Who knew but there might be girls at the Casa Carillo? Horrible thought!

The boys met a half hour later on the corridor, still

weak, but magnificent to look upon. Roldan's head was very high, despite his protesting knees: he felt himself again.

"It is the hour of siesta," he said. "Let us lie in these hammocks and wait. Ay! but it is warm, and the sky is blue, and the sun looks like the copper lamp of my mother - the one that came from Boston. Who - even an Indian - would live in the mountains when the valleys are so big and warm?"

They extended themselves in two hammocks swung across the corridor and watched the many doors on the several sides of the court. All were closed, and the forest had hardly been more quiet than the Casa Carillo in its hour of siesta. Through the arch of the gateway they could see the green of fields, a corner of a vineyard, and rolling hills. On either side of the entrance was a large magnolia-tree with broad shining leaves and bunches of cream-white fragrance. The oranges were very yellow, the palms very stately, the red tiles on the sloping roofs above the white walls looked very fresh and red. There was colour and beauty everywhere; and the boys were quite at peace, and content to be so. Their appetite for adventure was dulled for the moment.

Gertrude Atherton

XIV

A door on the opposite corridor opened and a youth came forth. He jerked his head diffidently at the guests and took the longest way round instead of crossing the court; but when he reached the boys, who were risen and awaiting him, he wore a dignified air of welcome, as befitted a young gentleman of his race.

"Welcome to Casa Carillo, senores," he said gravely. "The house is yours. Burn it if you will. I, myself, Rafael Carillo, am your slave."

To which Roldan replied: "We are at your feet, for you and yours have rescued us from death and given us food and clothing when we most needed it. Our lives are yours to do with as you wish."

"Then would we keep you here always, Don Roldan and Don Adan. All guests are welcome at Casa Carillo, but doubly those that need it."

Then, formalities over, as boys are pretty much alike the world round, Rafael was soon pouring forth eager questions, and our heroes were reliving the events of the past weeks. Arm in arm they strolled out into the wide beautiful valley, green with sprouting winter, the distant mountains of terrible memory quivering under a dark blue mist.

"Hist!" said Rafael, suddenly. "Do you know what day this is?"

"Day?" The adventurers had lost all count of time.

"It is the day before Christmas, my friends."

"No! Madre de dios!" Roldan and Adan stood still. For a moment they felt homesick. They saw the reproachful faces of their parents and brothers and sisters, to say nothing of visions of unclaimed presents. But Rafael gave them no time for regrets. He was the only child at home, and delighted with his new companions.

"To-morrow many people will come," he said. "I have ten married sisters and brothers. They all come from their ranchos, and many more. It will be very gay, my friends."

"Good," said Roldan, dismissing regret. "We will enjoy."

"And after Christmas is gone I know of something else," said Rafael, mysteriously. He glanced about. They stood in the midst of a great vineyard, each engaged upon a large purple bunch. "Come," said Rafael, with an air of mystery. "Not here. Some one may hide beneath the vines."

It was extremely unlikely, but the adventurers liked the suggestion and followed their host breathlessly into the open field. "One day in the summer," whispered Rafael, his eyes rolling about, "I went with four vaqueros with a present of venison to Father Osuna. He was not at the Mission, and a brother told us that he walked among the hills. I thought I would go to meet him and receive his blessing. For a time I saw no one, and I thought, 'Caramba! but the padre has long legs this hot weather!' Just then he stood before me. He had walked out of the side of the hill through a hole no wider than himself. He sweated like a bull after coliar, and his cassock was gathered in his two hands, leaving his bare shanks no more sacred than an Indian's. He did not look like a priest at all, and I forgot to kneel to him, but stared with my mouth open. And what do you think he did, my friends? He turned white like the hand of a dona in her teens and - and - dropped his cassock. And -"

"Well? well?"

"What do you think rolled to the ground, my friends? Chunks of yellow stuff that glittered, and a shower of sparkling yellow sand – beautiful as sunshine on the floor. I gave a cry and ran to pick it up. I had never seen anything so beautiful, I never had wanted anything so much. I felt that I would die for it in that moment, my friends. But that priest, what do you think he did? He gave a yell of rage, as if he could tear me in pieces, and flung himself all over that sunshine of earth. 'My gold!' he cried. 'Mine! mine! You shall not take it from me.' 'If it is yours it is not mine, my father,' I said, feeling ashamed, - though I still wanted it; 'I will help you to pick it up.' He got up then, his face very red again, and I could see that he was trying to put on his dignity as fast as he had put down his cassock - he looked better with both in place. 'My son,' he said,'the day is warm and I am very tired, and, I fear, a little ill. These rocks are nothing. They please my eye, and I pick them up sometimes as I walk among the hills. Leave them there. I do not want them. We will return to the Mission.' 'If you do not want them, then may I have them?' I asked - the blood flew all over my body, my friends. He scowled as if I had asked him for the candles on the altar. 'No,' he said, 'you cannot.' Then he put his big hand on my shoulder - he could twist your neck in a minute with those hands - 'Listen to me, my son,' he said, very soft, and looking so kind now, you can't think. 'There is poison in those stones, pretty as they are, deadly poison. It has murdered millions of souls and hundreds of bodies. Therefore I will not let you touch it - only a priest can touch it without ruining his soul. Therefore I forbid you - forbid you - ' he shouted this over me, 'to tell any one of what you have seen to-day. Neither your father nor your mother - no one. Do you understand?' I said 'Yes,' but I did not promise, and he was excited and did not notice. Then he dragged me away, and I looked about for other rocks that glittered. But there were none - not anywhere. And then I knew that they had come out of the hill; but I said nothing, and when we got back to the Mission and had had dinner and he was himself again and would have spoken alone with me, I ran and got on my horse, and all the brothers stood on the corridor to see me go. He came up to me and blessed me, and whispered: 'Tell no one, my son. If you do' - and he gave me a look that made my hair crackle at the roots. And to this day I have told no one. Did I tell my parents the priest would know in six hours. No boy has stayed here that I like. But now -"

"We will go to the hill and see for ourselves," said Roldan, promptly, and Adan gasped with horror and delight.

"Ay, I knew you would. I am brave, but I dared not go myself - that padre is too big. I wake up in the night and see his hands pawing in the air. But three of us -

we need fear no one."

"We will go as soon as the guests are gone. I have heard of this 'gold.' In Europe - I have an uncle who has travelled and has told me many things - bueno, in Europe, they make it into money and give it for things in big houses they call shops. Even here, in Monterey, and perhaps the other towns, they have a little - it comes from Mexico. My uncle said that one reason we were so happy was because we had so little money - none at all, we might say. That we got what we wanted out of the earth, or by trading with one another or with the skippers from Boston, who are glad to give us what we need from other lands in return for our hides and tallow. So, if we find this 'gold' perhaps we had better say nothing about it; but to find it - that will be a great, a grand adventure."

"We'll tell if we find it," said Adan, philosophically.

The boys concocted a plan of campaign to their satisfaction, then went home to supper. Don Tiburcio and his wife, Dona Martina, were already seated at the table in the big bare room. The grandee was a huge man with a soft profile, and cheeks as large and cream-hued as one of the magnolias hanging in the patio. He had an expression of indolent good-nature above his straight mouth, and long hands that looked lean and hard when they closed suddenly. He was a man of much influence in the politics of his country. His small-clothes were of dark green cloth with large silver buttons, the lace on his linen was fine and abundant. Dona Martina wore a gown of stiff flowered silk and a profusion of topaz ornaments. As the boys entered and bowed respectfully, Don Tiburcio eyed them keenly, but shook them cordially by the hand.

"So you are the son of Mateo Castanada," he said to Roldan. "It is evident enough, although you have something in the face that he has not. Otherwise I should not have done him to death in more than one political battle. Well, my sons, you are very welcome, and the longer you stay with us the better. The officers passed here some days ago - Rafael hid in the garret for the two days I feasted them, and they do not know that I have a son so young. Well, you are in good time to help my son enjoy his Christmas."

There was an abundant supper of meat with hot pepper-sauce, tomatoes and eggs baked together, and many dulces. The boys wondered if dried meat and coarse cakes were part of an adventurous dream.

The next morning chocolate was brought to the boys at half-past five, after which they dressed, and mounting the mustangs. awaiting their pleasure in the courtyard, went off for a morning canter. At Roldan's suggestion they reconnoitred the hills behind the Mission and got the bearings definitely shaped in their minds; the great raid was to be at night. They returned to a big breakfast at nine o'clock, then rode out again to meet the expected guests. It was but a few moments before they saw several cavalcades approaching from as many different directions. The young men and women, in silken clothes of every hue, were on horses caparisoned with velvet, carved leather, and silver; in many instances a girl had proud possession of the saddle, while her swain bestrode the anquera behind, his arm supporting her waist. Roldan wondered if anything would ever induce him to sacrifice his dignity like that. (It may be remarked here, as this history has only to do with the famous Californian's boyhood, that the day came when he could bow the knee to the fair sex with as graceful an ardour as did he not employ his sterner moments making laws and enforcing them.) The older folk travelled in carretas, the conveyance of the country, a springless wagon set on wheels cut from the solid thickness of the tree. It was driven by gananes, sitting astride the mustangs and singing lustily. The interior was lined with satin and padded, but was probably uncomfortable enough. Everybody looked smiling and happy, and a number of lads left their respective parties and cantered over to Rafael and his guests. A few moments later they all galloped at the top speed of their much-enduring mustangs to a great clump of oaks, where they dismounted and listened with breathless interest to the adventures of Roldan and Adan. All had been drafted, and must leave for barracks with the new year. They complimented the adventurers in a curious mixture of stately Spanish and eager youthfulness, and their admiration was so apparent that our heroes would have doubled the dangers of the past on the spot.

When they returned home to dinner the great space before the house was filled with shining horses pawing the ground under their heavy saddles. The court and corridors were an animated scene, overflowing with dons and donas in brilliant array. When dinner was over and the grown-up guests and young girls were lingering over the Christmas dulces, all the boys slipped away and went out to the huge kitchen, where countless Indian servants were busy or resting. They demanded four dozen eggs and help to blow them at once. The maids hastened to do the bidding of the little dons, and in less than a quarter of an hour the eggs were free of their natural contents, and all were busy refilling them with flour, or cologne, or scraps of gold and silver paper. Then the boys stuffed the fronts of their shirts, their sleeves, and their pockets with the eggs, and hid themselves among the palms of the court. Presently the guests came forth and scattered about the corridor, smiling and chatting in the soft subdued Spanish way. Suddenly twelve eggs, thrown with supple wrist and aimed with unfailing dexterity, flew through the air and crashed softly on the backs of caballeros' curls and donas' braids, flour powdering, gold and silver paper glittering on the dense blackness of those Californian tresses, cologne shooting down dignified spines. There was a chorus of shrieks, and then, as every head whisked about, and as a blow did not count unless it struck at the back, the boys ran up to the corridors, dodged under vengeful arms and continued the battle. Finally they were chased out into the open, and the guests having been provided with the remaining eggs by Dona Martina, the battle waged fierce and hot until, exhausted, the guests retired for siesta.

But siesta was brief that day. In less than an hour's time all had reappeared and were mounting for the race.

Gertrude Atherton

XV

The race took place in a field a mile from the house, on a straight track. Four vaqueros in black velvet small-clothes trimmed with silver, spotless linen, and stiff glazed black sombreros, walked up and down, leading the impatient mustangs. Two of these horses were a beautiful bronze-gold in colour, with silver manes and tails, a breed peculiar to the Californias; one was black, the other as white as crystal. The family and guests of Casa Carillo sat on their horses, in their carretas, or stood just outside the fence surrouncing the field. At one end were the several hundred Indians employed by Don Tiburcio, and several hundred more from the Mission. Father Osuna had also joined the party from the Casa, and Roldan, who had seen hundreds of horse-races and was built on a more complex plan than his contemporaries, got as close to the priest as he dared and gave him his undivided attention. Padre Osuna was a man of unusual height and heaviness of build. His black eyes were set close to his fine Roman nose. The mouth was so tightly compressed that its original curves were quite destroyed, and the intellectual development of the brow was very marked. His hands exerted a peculiar fascination over Roldan. They were of huge size, even for so big a man, lean and knotted, with square-tipped fingers. The skin on them was fine and brown; it looked as soft as a woman's. He used them a good deal when talking, and not ungracefully; but they seemed to claw and grasp the air, to be independent of the arms hidden in the voluminous sleeves of the smart brown cassock. Other people watched those hands too - they seemed to possess a magnetism of their own; and every one showed this priest great deference: he was one of the most successful disciplinarians in the Department of California, a brilliant speaker, an able adviser in matters of state, and a man of many social graces.

"More agreeable to meet in the sala of the Mission than in a cave at midnight," thought Roldan. "Still - " His scent for danger, particularly if it involved a matching of wits, was very keen.

The word was given. The race began. The dons shouted, the lovely faces between the bright folds of the rebosos flushed expectantly. From the black mass of Indians opposite came a mighty gurgle, which gradually broke into a roar, -

"The black! Fifty hides on the black!"

"The little bronze! She is a length ahead! Madre de dios! Six doubloons of Mexico on the little bronze!"

The priest pushed his way to the speaker, a wealthy ranchero who had been more than once to Mexico.

"The white against the bronze, senor," he said. "Twenty otter skins to the six doubloons of Mexico."

"Done, your reverence. I am honoured that you bet with me. But the white - have you thought well, my father?"

"She breathes well, and her legs are very clean."

"True, my father, but look at the muscles of the little bronze. How they swell! And the fire in the nostrils!"

"True, Don Jaime; and if she wins, the skins are yours."

As the horses darted down the track almost neck to neck, the excitement routed Spanish dignity. The dons stood up in their saddles, shouting and betting furiously. The women clapped their white idle hands, and cheered, and bet - but with less recklessness: a small jewel or a second-best mantilla. As they could not remember what they had bet when the excitement was over, these debts were never paid; but it pleased them mightily to make their little wagers. The men were betting ranchitas, horses, cattle, and, finally, their jewels and saddles and serapes. For each horse represented a different district of the Department, and there was much rivalry.

The priest did not shout, and he made no more bets, but his eyes never left those figures speeding like arrows from the bow, the riders motionless as if but the effigies of men strapped to the creatures of fire beneath. Sometimes the black gained then the little bronze; once the white dashed a full three yards beyond his fellows, and Roldan saw the great hands of the priest, which had been clinched against his shoulders, open spasmodically, then close harder than ever as the white quickly dropped back again.

It was a very close race. The excitement grew tense and painful. Even Roldan felt it finally, and forgot the priest. The big bronze had quite dropped out of it and was lagging homeward, hardly greeted by a hiss. The others were almost neck and neck, the little bronze slightly in the lead. "She wins," thought Roldan, "No! No! The black! the black! Ay, no, the bronze! but no! no! Ay! Ay! Ay!" A roar went up that ended in a shriek. The black had won.

Roldan looked at the priest. His skin was livid, his nostrils twitching. But his mouth and eyes told nothing.

The crowd rode home, still excited, gay, cheerful. Their losses mattered not. Were not their acres numbered by the hundred thousand? Did they not have more horses and cattle than they would ever count? In those days of pleasure and plenty, of luxury and unconsidered generosity, a rancho, a caponara the less, meant a loss neither to be felt nor remembered.

After the bountiful supper the guests loitered for a time in the courtyard, then the sala was cleared and the dance began. Several of the girls danced alone, while the caballeros clapped and shouted. Then all waltzed or took part in their only square dance, the contradanza. They kept it up until morning. Needless to say, our heroes went to bed at an early hour.

They were up the next morning with the dawn, and in company with Rafael and the other guests of their own age, went for their canter. This time they avoided the hills behind the Mission, as they had no wish to share their secret, and a chance word might divulge all. They rode toward the hills at the head of the valley. Roldan was still the hero of the hour, and Rafael, although the most generous of boys, resented it a little. He was not without ambitions of his own, and determined to seize the first opportunity to remind his companions that the son of Don Tiburcio Carillo, the greatest ranchero of that section of the Californias, had not the habit to occupy the humble position of tag-behind even to so brilliant and adventurous a guest as Roldan Castanada.

He soon found his opportunity.

As they reached the first hill they saw a bull feeding on its summit. "Aha!" cried the young don of the Rancho Encarnacion. "Now I will make for you a little morning entertainment, my friends. Coliar! coliar!"

"No! no!" cried the boys. "The hill is too steep. It is like the side of a house. You will break your neck, my friend."

Roldan said: "It is dangerous, but it could be done."

"I can do it," said Rafael, proudly, "and I shall."

The other boys, good sportsmen as they all were, shouted, "No! no!" again; but Rafael laughed gaily, and forced his horse up the almost perpendicular declivity, leisurely unwinding his lariat from the high pommel of his saddle, and tossing it into big snake-like loops, which he gathered one by one into his hand, the last about his thumb. The bull fed on unsuspecting. for the early green of winter was very delicious after eight months of unrelenting sunshine. When Rafael reached the summit he rode back for some distance, then came at the bull full charge, yelling like a demon. The bull, terrified and indignant, gave a mighty snort and leaped over the brow of the hill. It was much like descending the slightly inclined side of a cliff, but he kept his footing. The boys held their breath as Rafael rode straight over the brow in the wake of the bull. With one hand he held the bridle in a tight grip, in the other he held aloft the coils of the lariat. It looked like a huge snake, and quivered as if aware that it was about to spring. There was no cheering; the boys were too much alarmed. A mis-step and there would be a hideous heap at the foot of the hill.

The little mustang appeared scarcely to touch the uneven surface of the descent. He looked as if galloping in air, and tossed his head fiercely as though to shake the rising sun out of his eyes. The bull seemed continually gathering himself for a great leap, his clumsy bulk heaving from side to side. But a quarter of the distance had been traversed when the great curves of the lasso sprang forward, and, amidst a hoarse murmur from the boys, caught the bull below the horns. But that was all. The bull would not down! There would be no coliar! He merely ran on - the brute! the beast! - jerking his horns defiantly, putting down his head, nearly dragging Rafael from the saddle. But no! but no! Rafael has risen in his saddle, he has forced his mustang the harder, he is almost level with the bull - he has passed! He gives a great jerk, dragging the bull to his knees, then another, and the bull is on his side and rolling over and over down the hill, Rafael following fast, slackening his lariat. The boys now cheer wildly, although danger is not over - yes, in another moment it is, and Rafael, smiling complacently, is at the foot of the hill, disengaging the humbled bull.

"Bravo!" said a voice from behind the horses. All turned with a start. It was the priest. "Coliar was never better done," he added graciously; and Rafael felt that the day was his.

The priest had ridden up unnoted in the tense excitement of the last few moments. He sat a big powerful horse, and his bearing was as military as that of the two great generals of the Californias, Castro and Vallejo.

As the boys, congratulations and modest acknowledgement over, were making for home and breakfast, the priest pressed his horse close to Roldan's. "I interested you much at the race yesterday, Don Roldan," he said, with a good-humoured smile. "Why was that?"

Roldan was not often embarrassed, but he was so taken aback at the abrupt sally he forgot to be flattered that the priest had evidently thought it worth while to inquire his name; and stammered: "I - well, you see, my father, you are not like other priests." Which was not undiplomatic.

The priest smiled, this time with a faint flush of unmistakable pleasure. "You are right, my son, I am not as other priests in this wilderness. Would to Heaven I were, or -"

"Or that you were in Spain?" Roldan could not resist saying, then caught his breath at his temerity.

The priest turned about and faced him squarely. "Yes," he said deliberately, "and that I were a cardinal of Rome. Such words I have never uttered to mortal before; but if I am not as other men, neither are you as other lads. Some day you will be a Castro or an Alvarado; it is written in your face. Perhaps something more, for changes may come and your opportunities be greater. But I - I am no longer young; there is no hope in California for me."

"Why do you not return to Spain?"

"I have written. They will not answer. In my youth I was wild. They forced me to come here. I had no money. I was obliged to obey. I have christianized a few hundred worthless savages who were better off in their barbarism, and I have made myself a power among a few thousand men of whom the outer world, the great world, knows nothing. My Mission is the most prosperous in the Californias - and I -" he set and ground his teeth.

Roldan thought of the gold. "When I am governor of the Californias, my father," he said, "I shall send you back to Spain, for then I shall have great influence - and much gold."

At the last word the priest's eyes flamed with so fierce a light that Roldan shrank back repelled, feeling himself in the presence of a passion of which he had no knowledge. But the priest controlled himself at once. "Thank you, my son," he said with a brilliant smile. "And I do not ask you to guard as your own what I have said. It is a part of the power of such natures as yours that you know what to repeat and what to leave unsaid." Then as they approached the house he suddenly took Roldan's slender elegant hand in one of his mighty paws, shook it heartily, and flinging his bridle to a vaquero, sprang lightly to the ground and entered the courtyard, leaving our hero in a condition of flattered bewilderment.

Gertrude Atherton

XVI

That day there was to be a grand rodeo, or "round-up:" the branding of cattle; not only of the stock belonging to Don Tiburcio, but of many of his neighbours, which would be driven over to his rancho for the operation. This was one of the great occasions of the year. Immediately after breakfast the neighbours began to arrive, magnificently mounted, sparkling with gold and silver lace, their wives and daughters each surrounded by her cavalcade. About ten the gorgeous company, led by the host, started for an immense corral about three miles from the house. The boys were well to the front, and established themselves on the wall of the corral. The rest of the party remained on their horses, but mounted the little slopes. The green winter landscape had suddenly become a blaze of colour, and never was there a more animated scene. Over all hung a light haze. The distant mountains, which could be seen from the outer valley, were almost invisible. The priest, a huge brown figure, on his big brown horse, stood on the very apex of the highest knoll.

Presently, from various directions rose a low deep murmur, then a rumble of growing volume as of an approaching earthquake. Men and women grasped their bridles with firmer fingers, and pressed still nearer to the crests of the many mounds. Then over the hills on every side came a mass of tossing horns and sleek shining bodies, separated here and there by a shouting vaquero, whose black and silver seemed pierced at every point by those white curving horns. The cattle, several thousand in number, trotted over the hills and toward the corral swiftly, but in good order, held well in check by the careful vaqueros. There was no cheering, for excitement was to be avoided. The cattle would stand any amount of the shouting they were used to, but little from unaccustomed throats.

In the corral, at its farther end, stood, by an oven, a tall muscular Indian, the most famous brander in that part of the country. He was stripped to the waist, and as the first steer was driven through the narrow gate, he plucked a red-hot iron from the coals. The beast, kicking and bellowing, was flung to the ground by a dexterous twist of his tail, two more Indians held him in position, and the branding was accomplished.

Almost before he was up another was prostrate; and they followed each other in such rapid succession that the wonder was some were not branded twice. As fast as each brute received his mark he was driven out of another gate and over the hills, lest his ill-nature should be the cause of wild disorder.

The vaqueros handled their dangerous charges with admirable skill, keeping those to be branded in groups of a hundred or more at some distance from the corral, riding round them constantly with peremptory shouts. Other vaqueros, belonging to the same herd, segregated the animals immediately required and drove them in a straight line for the corral. There was not a moment of pause. The vaqueros, the brander, and his assistants seemed impervious to fatigue; the cattle, shifting uneasily in their bands, leaped eagerly from the lines at the first signal from the vaquero bearing down on them like a fury from the corral. On the far side, otherwise deserted, the sore indignant beasts scampered as fast as their legs could carry them whithersoever their vaquero chose to drive.

After two hours or more, the atmosphere was charged with a certain breathless excitement, as was natural enough. The constant cyclonic rush of vaqueros and cattle, the angry bellowings, the increasing masses of animals, the furious shouts of the men, had changed a peaceable landscape into a vast theatre full of tragic possibilities. The waiting cattle were growing more and more restless, and there was a low rumble among them. Don Tiburcio motioned to his guests that it was time to leave; moreover, it was nearing the dinner hour.

"Rafael!" he called. His son turned his head impatiently, but prepared to obey; the Californian youth was brought up on rigid lines.

"Ay, must we go?" cried Adan. "I could stand here till night, even without dinner, my friends."

"I, too, am sorry," began Roldan. "But what is the matter?"

The great masses of cattle had begun to heave suddenly. They were uttering hoarse growls of terror. The mustangs of the vaqueros stood suddenly still, quivering. Then, abruptly, a horrible stillness fell. All things breathing seemed to petrify. But only for numbered seconds. From beneath came a low roar, gathering in volume like the progression of a tidal wave; then the world heaved and rocked.

"Temblor! temblor!" went up as from one mighty horrified throat. The priest shouted to the boys: "Stay where you are;" to Don Tiburcio and his guests: "With all your speed after me."

They understood his meaning. The cattle were leaping over one another, bellowing madly, giving no heed to the hoarse cries of the terrified vaqueros. In a moment a blaze of colour was flying down the valley, a long brown arm lifted high above it. In twenty seconds five thousand tossing horns and blazing eyes and heaving flanks were in pursuit.

The vaqueros did their best, although their faces were white and their lips shaking. Three that were between the uniting herds, had their legs crushed into their mustangs' sides, and were borne along and aloft, shrieking horribly, adding to the fury of the stampede. Another, trying to head the cattle off, rode into a sudden split in the hard adobe soil and went down beneath those iron feet.

The boys clung together. The wall was broad, but it rocked continuously, whether from other shocks or from the hoof-assaulted earth it would have been impossible to say. A curving outer flank of the flying mass bulged against it, and it quivered horribly with the impact. The boys strained their eyes after the retreating points of colour. Would they escape? Were the frightened mustangs fleeter of foot than those maddened brutes? And if they were - the Casa!

"I think," said Roldan, "that we had better get down on the other side. This wall may go down any minute; and the cattle are all looking in one direction."

"You are right," said Rafael. "This way - Ay de mi!"

There was another heave of the earth, distinct from the steady vibration of stampeding cattle. The adobe wall rocked violently, sprang, twisted, crumbled to the ground, a heap of dust.

For a moment the boys were invisible. Then they emerged, one by one, choking and spitting, rubbing their eyes with their knuckles. When they had recovered some measure of vision they huddled together, staring with affrighted eyes at the moving wall of cattle not twenty yards to their left, hardly able to keep their balance.

Suddenly Roldan pulled his wits together. "Sit down," he said. "We are the colour now of the earth. If we keep quiet and look no taller than weeds they will not see us and we shall not be hurt."

The boys dropped to the ground and sat in silence, staring ahead of them. Would that rushing, heaving, bellowing mass have no end? It was indeed a long time before the last line, curiously compact, swept by. Occasionally the earth jumped with brief abruptness, causing hair to crackle at the roots, and dust-laden as it was, make as if to rise on end. The squirrels were screeching in the trees. The birds pitifully twittered. Even the leaves rustled in response to those terrible quivers.

The cattle were a red streak at the end of the perspective. The boys rose, shook themselves, and walked heavily to their tethered mustangs. The poor beasts were trembling and whinnying; they greeted their young masters with a quavering neigh of relief.

The boys mounted; but although they rode rapidly, with ever increasing impatience, they paused every few moments to listen; there was likely to be a return stampede at any moment. More than once they were obliged to swerve suddenly aside from yawning rifts, and they passed a spring of boiling water, spouting and hissing upward, which had not been there in the morning. They were too frightened to talk; not only the paralysing awe of the earthquake was upon them, but the least imaginative saw his home levelled to the ground, his relatives and friends trodden down into the cracking earth. Hills lay between them and the Casa Encarnacion.

There were two exits from the valley where the branding had taken place: one, very narrow, to the right, which led directly to the house, the other straight ahead, almost as broad as the valley itself. The boys saw at a glance that pursued and pursuers had taken the more spacious way, and they followed without consultation.

The crushed grass looked like green blood, but there was no other evidence of slaughter; the mustangs had been fleeter than the cattle. The latter had evidently kept well together, for on either side of a swath some three hundred yards in width, the grass stood high.

They were in a wide valley now; they could see the great mountains, still faint under their vapourous mist, the redwoods as rigid of outline as if the heart of the world beneath had never changed its measure. Just beyond this valley was a wood, then the Mission. Were twenty thousand hoofs trampling among its ruins?

They left the valley, entered the wood, galloped down

its narrow path, and emerged. The Mission stood on its plateau above the river, as serene and proud as the redwoods on the mountain. She had held her own against many earthquakes and would against many more. But there was not a horn, a horse, a man, nor a woman to be seen.

The boys dismounted, not daring to think. They walked toward the buildings, then paused to listen. Through the open doors of the church rolled the sonorous tones of Padre Osuna's voice, intoning mass. The boys ran forward to enter the building. They paused on the threshold, held by a sight, the like of which had never been seen in California before, and never shall be again.

Near the entrance of the vast building were a multitude of half-clothed dusky forms, prone. Between them and the altar were more than an hundred horses, caparisoned with silver and carved leather, and gay anquera. They stood as if petrified. On them, huddled to the arching necks, in an attitude of prostrate devotion, were magnificent bunches of colour; scarce an outline could be seen of the proudly attired men and women who had fled before a tidal wave of tossing horns. Father Osuna, in his coarse brown woollen robes, stood before the altar, chanting the mass of thanksgiving. The church blazed with the light of many candles. The air was thick and sweet with incense.

XVII

After the mass was over the boys learned the sequel of the morning's terrible adventure. Between the second valley and the wood the cattle, diverted by one of those mysterious impulses which govern masses of all grades of intelligence, had deflected suddenly and raced for the hills. The gay company was much shaken, but somewhat restored by the calm of the church and the solemn monotonous roll of Father Osuna's voice. They cantered slowly homeward, and crossed themselves fervently when they saw the Casa Encarnacion none the worse for her shaking, beyond a few fallen tiles. After dinner and siesta they recovered their natural spirits, and the men and boys went forth with the vaqueros to hunt the cattle. These were found at the foot of the mountain, weary and humble. Not a horn was tossed in defiance at the volley of abuse hurled upon them, and they allowed themselves to be driven to the ranches of their respective owners without a protest.

That evening the household and guests of Casa Encarnacion spent in music and dancing; so light of heart and careless of mind were the people of that time and country.

A number of cattle had been trampled to death in the stampede, and the bodies lay within a few miles of the mountains. It was inevitable that bears would come out to eat the carcasses. On the night of the day of terrifying memory no one felt equal to the exertion of another ten mile ride and the subsequent battle with a possible herd of bears. But at eight o'clock on the following night Don Tiburcio, Padre Osuna, the boys, some ten of the caballeros, and as many vaqueros mounted and rode forth for a good night's sport. The moon was thin and low. As they approached the spot where the first of the wild band had succumbed to fatigue they saw a dark object moving beside the carcass. The approach was stealthy, but the bear suddenly raised his head. In a second five or six lassos had sprung through the air. One caught the bear - a brown bear of moderate size - about the neck, another about a hind leg. The brute drew his legs together like a bucking horse and leaped into the air, then plunged toward his tormentors; but those that had him in lasso galloped in different directions, and poor bruin was quickly strained and strangled to death. Two vaqueros were left to skin him, and the party rode on. In a very few moments they saw a moving group some distance ahead. Spurring their mustangs they dashed forward, letting the lassos fly. Now the sport became truly exciting and dangerous. Some six or eight brown bears, of varying sizes, growled furiously and bounded toward the intruders. Three were caught in the meshes of the rope, the others were making straight for the horses. There was only one thing to do. The men put spurs and galloped rapidly away, the bears plunging heavily in pursuit. When the men had outdistanced the bears by a hundred yards or more, they wheeled suddenly and trotted back, once more letting fly the lasso. This time all but one were roped; as they kicked in fury, their hind legs were caught by the lariats held in reserve; and there followed a scene of plunging and springing, galloping, shouting, growling; and neighing, for the mustangs were fully alive to their part.

The one bear at liberty rode straight for Roldan.

He had hurled his lasso with the rest, and it was trailing. He jerked about and fled for a mile or more, holding on with his legs while both hands were occupied gathering in the rope and coiling it about the high pommel of his saddle. Then he turned and charged full at the bear, who was hot in pursuit and no mean runner. He hurled the lariat. It fell short, and lay quivering on the ground like a huge wounded snake. Roldan gave an exclamation, of surprise as much as of dismay: he was an expert with the rope. He turned, however, dragging it in. It caught about the mustang's hind legs. The beast went down, neighing with horror. Roldan tried to jerk him to his feet. He seemed hopelessly entangled. Roldan extricated himself, knowing that he was comparatively safe, as bears prefer horse-meat to man's. He had no sooner got his feet free of the boots than the mustang leaped to his feet and fled like a hare, dragging the lariat in a straight line after him.

Roldan was alone, the bear not ten yards away. The rest of his party were a mile and more behind. No one apparently had noticed his flight with the solitary bear. The light was uncertain and the excitement over there intense.

Roldan took to his agile young heels. But the bear gathered himself and leaped, not once but several times. There was no doubt that his blood was up, and that he meant a duel to the death. Roldan turned with a catching of what breath was left in him. He

Gertrude Atherton

mechanically drew his knife from its pocket and flourished it at the advancing bear. Bruin cared as little for steel as for rope. He came on with a mighty growl.

Roldan gave one rapid glance about. There was not even a tree in sight. From his point of departure an object seemed approaching, but it was too dark to tell as yet whether it was a horseman or another bear. The brute was almost on him, panting mightily. All the senses between Roldan's skeleton and his skin concentrated in the determination to live. He sprang forward and plunged his long knife into the protruding injected eye of the bear, then leaped aside, his dripping knife in his hand, and danced about the maddened beast with the agility of a modern prize-fighter. The bear, too, danced, as if obsessed by some infernal music; and the skipping, and leaping, and dodging, and waltzing of these two would have been ludicrous had it not been a matter of life and horrid death. Through it all Roldan was vaguely conscious of approaching hoofbeats, but there was no room in his consciousness for hope or despair. He was not even aware that he was panting as if his lungs and throat were bursting, nor even that his vision was a trifle blurred from constant and rapid change of focus and surcharged veins. But he executed his dance of life as unerringly as if fresh from his bed and bath. The bear, a clumsy creature at best, and streaming and blinded with his blood, was slackening a little, but there was life in him yet, and twice its measure of vengeance. Suddenly he lay down, but became so abruptly inert that Roldan was not deceived. Instead of putting himself within reach of those waiting arms he fled with all his strength. It was then that he knew how fully that strength was spent: his lungs and legs refused to work with his will and impulse after the first hundred yards, and he fell to the ground with a sensation of utter indifference, longing only for physical rest. He heard the bear plunging after, the loud sound of a horse's hoofs, mingled with a single shout, then gave up his consciousness.

He awoke in a few moments. Adan was bending over him, propping his head. "The bear?" he demanded, ashamed of the pitiful quality of his voice.

"I came just in time to rope him," replied Adan. "You were a fool, my friend, to go off alone like that - but very brave," he added hastily, knowing that Roldan did not like criticism.

"You are quite right. And this is the second time you and your lariat have saved me. Perhaps it may be the other way some time."

"Likely it will if you go on hunting for adventures as the old women hunt for fleas of a night. Do you feel able to get on my horse? It will carry the two of us."

"If I were not equal to that much I should find another bear and go to sleep in his arms."

Gertrude Atherton

XVIII

At last the night arrived for the gold quest. The guests had gone. Roldan, Adan, and Rafael were alone on their side of the great house. They waited, kicking their heels together with leashed impatience, until eleven o'clock. The family and servants of Casa Encarnacion went to bed at ten o'clock, but it was the custom of Don Tiburcio to go the rounds a half or three quarters of an hour later and see that his strict laws were as strictly obeyed. To-night, when he opened the doors of the three young dons in succession, heels were still, and breathing was as monotonous as his own would be an hour later. At eleven the boys dressed and swung from their windows, not daring to leave by the courtyard. Nor did they dare go to the corral and abstract three horses. Much to their distaste, for there was nothing the Californian hated so much as to travel on two legs, they were obliged to walk the miles between the Casa and the hills. But their legs were young and their brains eager; in little over an hour they were in sight of the Mission.

It looked very white and ghostly in the pale blaze of the moon, a huge mass, full of prayer and discontent. Close beside it, but without the walls, the Indians slept in the rancheria, quiescent enough, for they had no Anastacio. At midnight the great bells in the tower had rung out, filling the valley with their sweet silver clamour; but as the boys approached and skirted the wall, some distance to the right, the Mission might have been as lifeless as it is this year, in its desertion and decay.

The hills were a mile behind. The Mission, like all of its kind, stood on a broad open, that no hostile tribe might approach unseen. Cows and horses lay in their first heavy sleep, their breathing hardly ruffling the profound stillness. So great an air of repose did the silent walls and sleeping beasts give to the landscape that the boys felt the quiet of the night as they had not done in the other valley, and drew closer together, almost holding their breath lest the priests might hear it. A quarter of an hour later they were among the hills and standing before the aperture whose secrets were known only to Padre Osuna. They glanced at each other out of the corners of their eyes. Brave as they were, they did not altogether like the idea of a possible encounter with a rattlesnake or a bear in the dark and narrow confines of a cave. And if there should be another earthquake! However, they had not come to turn back, and Roldan pushed boldly in, the others following close.

For a time their way lay along a narrow passage. They had made two abrupt turns before they dared to light the lantern they had brought. When Rafael did, it revealed nothing but earthy walls and the imprint of feet on the ground. After a little, however, the passage suddenly widened, and it was Adan who uttered the first exclamation of surprise. It was, indeed, a hoarse gurgle. The walls were veined with what appeared to be irregular bands of dirty crystal, pricked with glittering yellow. There were, perhaps, a thousand of these little points bared from the jealous earth, and they shone with a steady baleful glare, magnetising six youthful eyes, stirring in three careless brains the ghosts of ancient gold-lust, whose concrete substance lay in the marble vaults of Spain. Immediately Roldan's sympathy went out to the priest; and he knew that that commanding intelligence could teach him one thing the less.

There was a rough pick on the ground, and many junks of quartz. Roldan struck and rubbed two pieces together. In a moment his palm was filled with jagged pieces of yellow metal. He blew on them lovingly, then put them in his pocket.

"Dios de mi alma!" gasped Rafael, whose eyes were bulging from his head. "It is as beautiful as the stars of the sky, - the stars in the milky way with the film over them."

"But we need no more stars," said Adan. "We shall take away our pockets full, but what shall we do with it? Surely this was not made to rot with the earth. But it is too small for what you call money, if that is so big as you say, Roldan. It would make fine nails for a church door."

"Now is not the time to think what you will do with it," said Roldan. "It is enough that we have it to get. Much is very loose in the crystal. Rub free all that you can, and fill every pocket. We will take all we can carry away, and come again and again. Some day, when we are men, perhaps, we will find a use for it. I for one do not believe that anything that makes you love it can do harm. Does not the Church teach us to love all things? Now let us work and not talk."

The boys in turn hacked out great pieces of quartz and rubbed the free gold loose. Much of it could only be crushed out in machinery made for the purpose, but a sufficient quantity of the quartz was poor and soft. As the boys worked, they grew more and more silent, more and more absorbed. They forgot their delight in rodeo, coliar, bear-hunts, bull-fights, riding about the ranches from morning till noon, the race, the religious processions, the dulces of their mothers' cooks. A new and mighty passion possessed them, the strongest they had ever known. Their lips were pressed hard together - those soft Spanish lips that were usually half apart - their eyes glowed with a steady fire. Their chests rose and fell in short regular spasms.

Suddenly a thrill ran through Roldan. He had felt it before when a rattlesnake, ready to strike, had fixed its green malignant eyes upon him. He flashed the lantern about swiftly, twisting his neck with deep anxiety. It would be no minor adventure to encounter a coiled rattler in this narrow place. Then he saw something white shining out of the darkness high above the rays, a large white disk, in which glittered two points of light inexpressibly infuriate.

Roldan sprang to his feet with a warning cry. The other boys, greed routed by the danger sense, were on their feet as quickly. As the three lads, none very tall for his age, faced the gigantic bulk of the priest, they looked cornered and helpless.

The priest, unconsciously beyond doubt, lifted his huge hands, opening and shutting them slowly. The movement had an ugly significance, and the hands, in the miserable glimmer of light, looked like great bats, and seemed to pervade the cavern. Involuntarily the boys

Gertrude Atherton

squirmed. Then Roldan, mindful always of his proud position as captain of his small band, stepped in front of that band and spoke with a vocal control that did him much credit, considering that his heart seemed to be kicking in the middle of his stomach.

"These hills are just beyond the Mission grant, Padre Osuna," he said. "Nor are they on any rancho. Therefore what is in them is as much ours as any man's. This is the first time that we have been here, but it will not be the last; and when I am the governor of all the Californias, I shall send many Indians to dig the very heart out of these hills. So pick out all that you can now, Padre Osuna, for ten years hence -"

As he spoke fear gave place to exultation in finding himself pitted against a man whom he intuitively respected more than any he had ever met, and whom he knew most men feared and none understood. Moreover, he heard two sets of teeth clattering behind him, and that alone would have sent the blood of a born leader of men back to its skin.

But his speech did not proceed to the finish. The priest swooped down and caught the three necks between his hands, easily spanning them, pressing the heads hard together. Then he lifted the boys high in the air and held them there, a kicking, humiliated trio. The blanched olive of his face was reflected in the pallid brows at the extremity of his rigid arms. His voice, which had been lost in passion, found itself.

"And when your Indians come, Senor Don Roldan," he said, "they will find three skeletons six feet beneath the floor of this cave. You will never leave this cave, not one of you. When you are dead for want of food and drink, I shall return and bury you. And no one will seek you here." Suddenly he dashed them to the ground. "A thousand curses go with you," he shrieked, "to make a murderer of me. I was near enough to hell before -"

"And our fingers will scratch the ground beneath your feet," interrupted Roldan, who between mortification and rage felt equal himself to murder, but determined as ever to hold his own. "Our skulls will grin at you from every corner as you work -"

"I don't care!" shouted the priest. "I don't care! Here you rot. This gold is mine. No man shall touch it but myself."

"But if we promise never to return, and to tell no man of what we know," interposed Rafael, feebly.

The priest laughed. "With the glitter of gold in your brains? You could not keep an oath on the cross." He turned swiftly and strode down the passage.

"What will he do?" gasped Adan.

"Roll a stone over the entrance and secure it with others," said Roldan. "There are plenty nigh. If we follow, he will beat us back with those fists, and one blow would crack our skulls in two."

"Then what shall we do? Rot here? Starve to death? Madre de dios!"

"We have been between the teeth of death before, have we not? We shall have many more adventures, my friends."

But although he spoke confidently he was profoundly disturbed. This was no ordinary predicament. He knew that unless the priest relented they stood small chance of seeing sun and stars again. Would he relent? Roldan's own indomitable will and growing ambitions responded to the awful forces in the man, overgrown and abnormal as they had become. That the priest had some great end in view to which this gold was the means, and that the gold itself had roused in him a controlling passion, he could not doubt. The priest himself had told him something, the gold the rest. With a sudden impulse of hatred Roldan emptied his pockets of the metal and stamped upon it. He quieted suddenly, then stamped again, with added vigour. Then he dropped and laid his ear to the ground.

"Stamp, Adan," he said, "and hard."

Adan shook his blood through his veins, and obeyed. Roldan sprang to his feet. "We are above the tunnel of the Mission," he said. "And we have a pickaxe. All we have to do is to dig."

XIX

It was three hours later that a mass of loosened earth caved suddenly, carrying Adan with it. A wild yell came back. It stopped abruptly, the tag end of it shot forth like the quick last blast from a trumpet.

"Hi, Adan!" called Roldan, excitedly, peering down into the dark. "Are you hurt?"

"I know not! I know not! It is darker than a dungeon of a Mission." The voice was quite distinct. It came from no great depth.

"Get out of the way," called Roldan. "I am coming." He waited a moment, then dropped, falling on a mass of soft earth. Adan had prudently retreated a few steps. He ran forward and helped Roldan to his feet, just as Rafael came flying down.

"Now for the other end," said Roldan. "This air is not too good. And that devil may return any moment."

They ran down the tunnel. It was wide and high, built for flying priests, should the Mission be besieged and captured by savage tribes. The air was close and heavy, but free from noxious gases. Bats whirred past and rats scampered before them. Roldan paused after a moment and lit his lantern. Its thin ray leaped but a few feet

Gertrude Atherton

ahead, but would frighten away any wild beast of the forest that might have wandered in.

The tunnel was straight. It also appeared to be endless.

"We have walked twenty leagues," groaned Adan, at the end of an hour.

"Two," said Roldan. "Without doubt this tunnel ends at the mountains, and they are four leagues from the Mission. But you have taken longer walks than this, my friend. Do you remember that night in the mountains?"

"I had forgotten it for one blessed week. Rafael, to what have we brought you? Your poor muscles are soft, where ours are now as hard as a deserter's from an American barque - ay, yi!"

"If they have but the chance to become soft once more after they too are hard!" muttered Rafael, who was panting and lagging. "That priest! that priest!"

"It is true," said Roldan, pausing abruptly. "You will not dare to return home at present - nor we. It is flight once more - to Los Angeles. We will stay there - where he would not dare touch us if he came - until he repents or makes sure that we will have told if we intend to tell. Will you come?"

"Will I? I would go to Mexico if I could. I feel that there is not room in the Californias for those hands and myself."

"I will take care of you," said Roldan, proudly, anxious to rout the memory of his recent humiliation. "But come." And Rafael, too weary and bewildered to resent the authority of his erst-while rival, trudged obediently in the rear.

"It grows colder," said Adan, significantly.

"Yes," said Roldan. "We near the mountains."

Adan stopped. "Is it the mountains again?" he asked. "If it is, then I, for one, prefer the priest."

"The mountains never scared you half as badly as the priest did," said Roldan, cruelly. "And to say nothing of the fact that we need never get lost in the mountains again, the embrace of a grizzly would be no harder and more death-sure than one in the great arms of that fiend that wears a cassock."

"True. You are always right. But promise that whatever happens you will not lead us into the Sierras."

"I promise," said Roldan, much flattered by this unconscious tribute to his leadership.

"Do you think that priest is really a devil?" asked Rafael, in an awestruck voice.

"When a man has insulted you, you do not know what you think of him," said Roldan, flushing hotly. "If he only were not a priest I'd fight him, big as he is. But at least I can outwit him. It consoles me to think of his fury when he goes to the cave and finds us gone."

"We'd better get out of this tunnel before we talk about having the best of the priest," said Adan. "Suppose he

Gertrude Atherton

returns to kill us himself -"

"He will not return until to-morrow. Then he will have repented. He will promise to let us go free if we keep his secret. But he will not have that satisfaction, my friends. Yesterday he had a friend in Roldan Castanada; I would have done anything for him, gladly kept his secret. But to-day he has an enemy that he will do well to fear. A Spaniard never forgets an insult."

"What shall you do?" asked Rafael, eagerly. "Expose him?"

"No, I do nothing mean. But I proclaim at Los Angeles that gold has been discovered in the Californias, and in six days the hills will swarm, and the priest in his cell will gnash his teeth."

"Ay!" exclaimed Adan. "Do you feel that?"

An icy blast swept down the tunnel, roughening skin and shortening breath. A few moments later the low rhythm as of distant water came to their ears. Roldan and Adan recognised that familiar music, and set their teeth.

"And I prayed that I might never see another redwood," muttered Adan, crossing himself.

The tunnel stopped abruptly. They stood before a mass of brushwood, piled thickly to keep out wild beasts and delude the searching eye of hostile Indians. Beyond, seen in patches, was a dazzle of white.

"Snow, of course," said Adan, with a groan.

The boys pulled the branches apart without much difficulty: the priests had studied facility of egress and had raised the barrier from within. In a few moments the boys stood in the sunlight; and the mountains hemmed them in.

Adan stamped his foot savagely on the hard snow. "We are where we started a week ago," he said. "No more, no less."

"No," said Roldan, who also had felt demoralised for a moment. "The priests were too clever for that. They would want to get into the shelter of the mountains, no more. I believe that from the top of that point above the tunnel we can see the valley."

"Well, we can at least look," said Rafael, who was bitterly weary and hungry, but determined not to be outdone by these hardened adventurers.

The boys made their way up the declivity as best they could through the heavy snowdrifts, pulling themselves up by clutching at young trees and scrub. They were thinly clad and very cold, and hunger was loud of speech. When after a half-hour's weary climb, they reached the summit, they drew a long sigh of relief, but their enthusiasm was too moderate for words in present physical conditions. The valley lay below. Far away, beyond leagues of low hills and wide valleys something white reflected the sun. It was the Mission.

"We have not a moment to rest, unless we can find a safe hiding-place," said Roldan. "If he should return and find us gone, he would follow at once."

"Where shall we go?" asked the others, who, however,

felt a quickening of blood and muscle at the thought that the priest might be under their feet even then.

"How near is the next rancho, and whose is it?"

"A league beyond the Mission grant. It is Don Juan Ortega's."

"Very well, we go there and ask for horses."

The boys made their way rapidly down the slope, which after all was only that of a foot-hill. Beyond were other foot-hills, and they skirted among them, finally entering a canon. It was as dark and cold and damp as the last hour of the tunnel had been, but the narrow river, roaring through its middle, had caught all the snow, and there was scarce a fleck on the narrow tilted banks. The hill opposite was the last of the foot-hills; but how to reach it? The current was very swift, and boys knew naught of the art of swimming in that land of little water.

Suddenly Roldan raised his hand with an exclamation of surprise and pointed to a ledge overhanging the stream. A hut stood there, made of sections of the redwood and pine. From its chimney, smoke was curling upward.

The boys were too hungry to pause and reflect upon the possibility of a savage inmate; they scrambled up the bank and ran along the ledge to the hut. The door was of hide. They knocked. There was no response. They flung the door aside and entered. No one was in the solitary room of the hut, but over a fire in the deep chimney place hung a large pot, in which something of agreeable savour bubbled.

Roldan glanced about. "I'd rather be invited," he said doubtfully.

But Adan had gone straight for the pot. He lifted it off the fire, fetched three broken plates and battered knives and forks from a shelf, and helped his friends and himself. Then he piously crossed himself and fell to. It was not in human necessities to withstand the fragrance of that steaming mess of squirrel, and the boys had disposed of the entire potful before they raised their eyes again. When they did, Rafael, who sat opposite the door, made a slight exclamation, and the others turned about quickly. A man stood there.

He was quite unlike any one they had ever seen. A tall lank man with rounded shoulders, lean leather-like cheeks, a preternatural length of jaw, drab hair and chin whiskers, and deeply-set china-blue eyes, made up a type uncommon in the Californias, that land of priest, soldier, caballero, and Indian. He was clad in coyote skins, and carried a gun in his hand, a brace of rabbits slung over one shoulder. He did not speak for some seconds, and when he did, it was to make a remark that was not understood. He said: "Well, I'll be durned!"

His expression was not forbidding, and Roldan recovered himself at once. He stood up and bowed profoundly.

"Senor," he said, "I beg that you will pardon us. We would have craved your hospitality had you been here, but as it was, our hunger overcame us: we have not eaten for many hours. But I am Roldan Castanada of the Rancho de los Palos Verdes, senor, and I beg that you will one day let me repay your hospitality in the house of my fathers."

"Holy smoke!" exclaimed the man, "all that high-falutin' lingo for a potful of squirril. But you're welcome enough. I don't begrudge anybody sup." Then he broke into a laugh at the puzzled faces of his guests, and translated his reply into very lame Spanish. The boys, however, were delighted to be so hospitably received, and grinned at him, warm, replete, and sheltered.

The man began at once to skin a rabbit. "Seein' as how you haint left me nothin', I may as well turn to," he said. "And it ain't every day I'm entertainin' lords."

The boys did not understand the words, but they understood the act, and reddened.

"I myself will cook the rabbit for you, senor," said Adan.

"Well, you kin," and the man nodded acquiescence.

"You are American, no?" asked Roldan.

"I am, you bet."

"From Boston, I suppose?"

The man guffawed. "Boston ought to hear that. She'd faint. No, young 'un, I'm not from no such high-toned place as Boston. I'm a Yank though, and no mistake. Vermont."

"Is that in America?"

"In Meriky? Something's wrong with your geography, young man. It's one of the U. S. and no slouch, neither."

He spoke in a curious mixture of English and of Spanish that he adapted as freely as he did his native tongue. The boys stared at him, fascinated. They thought him the most picturesque person they had ever met.

"When did you come?" asked Roldan.

"I'll answer any more questions you've got when I've got this yere rabbit inside of me. P'r'aps as you've been hungry you know that it doesn't make the tongue ambitious that way. I'll have a pipe while it's cookin'."

He was shortly invisible under a rolling grey cloud. The tobacco was the rank stuff used by the Indians. The boys wanted to cough, but would have choked rather than be impolite, and finally stole out with a muttered remark about the scenery.

When they returned their host had eaten his breakfast and smoked his second pipe.

"Come in," he said heartily. "Come right in and make yourselves ter home. My name's Jim Hill. I won't ask yourn as I wouldn't remember them if I did. These long-winded Spanish names are beyond me. Set. Set. Boxes ain't none too comfortable, but it's the best I've got."

"Oh, this box is most comfortable," Roldan hastened to assure him. "And we are very thankful to have anything to sit on at all, senor. You could not guess the many terrible adventures we have had in the last few weeks."

"Indeed! Adventures? I want ter know! You look as if hammocks was more to your taste. Oh, no offence," as Roldan's eyes flashed. "But you are fine looking birds, and no mistake. Howsomever, we'll hear all about them presently. It's polite to answer questions first. You was asking me a while back how I come here. I come over those mountains, young man, and I don't put in the adjectives I applied to them in the process outer respect to your youth. But they'd make a man swear if he'd spent his life psalm singin' before."

"We know," said Roldan, grimly. "We've been in them. What did you eat? And did you get lost?"

"I ate red ants mor' 'n once, and I usually was lost. When I arrived at that Mission down yonder the amount of flesh I had between my bones and my skin wouldn't have filled a thimble. But that priest - he's a great man if ever there was one - soon fixed me up. I lived like a prince for a month, and I could be there yet if I liked, but I'd kinder got used to livin' alone and I liked it, so I come here. Besides, I found so much prayin' and bell ringin' wearin' on the nerves, to say nothin' of too many Indians. I ain't got no earthly use for Indians. Why priests or anybody else run after Indians beats me. Where I was brought up 't was the other way. They're after us with a scalpin' knife, and if we're after them at all it's with all the lead we kin git. If the murderin' dirty beasts is willin' to stay where they belong, well, I for one believe in lettin' 'em."

"Do you - ah - like the priest, Don Jim?"

"What? Well, that's better than 'Don Himy,' as they call me down there. You bet I like the priest. He's a gentleman, and as square as they make 'em, that is, with a poor devil like me; I guess he's one too much for your dons when he feels that way. But he's a man every inch of him, afraid of nothin' under God's heaven, and as kind and generous as a - as some women. What he rots in this God-forsaken place for I can't make out."

"What did you come to California for?"

"Well, that ain't bad. I come here, my son, because I was lookin' for a cold climate. My own was warm, accordin' to my taste, and somehow Californy seemed as if it ought to be fur enough away to be cool and nice."

"It's very hot in the valleys."

"So it is. So it is. But as you see, I prefer the mountains."

"Do you often go to the Mission?"

"Every month or so I go down and have a chin with Padre Osuna. It keeps my Spanish in, and I shouldn't like to lose sight of him. I got word from him the other day that he wanted to see me mighty particular, and I'm wonderin' what's in the wind. Maybe you heard him say."

"No," said Roldan; but he guessed.

"Now," said Hill, "spin your yarn. I'm just pinin' to hear those adventures."

Roldan appreciated the sarcasm, but was too secure in the wealth of the past month to resent it. He began at the beginning and told the story with his curious combination of reserve and dramatic fire. As he had already told it several times it ran glibly off his tongue and had several inevitable embellishments. The man, whose cold blue eyes had wandered at first, finally fixed themselves on Roldan; and his whole face gradually softened. When Roldan finished with his and Adan's rescue by Don Tiburcio's vaquero, he held out his hand and said solemnly, -

"Shake."

Roldan allowed his hand to be gripped by that hairy paw; he was too elated to resent it as a familiarity.

"You've got pluck," continued Hill, "and I respect pluck mor' 'n anything else on earth. You're a man and a gentleman, and Californy'll be proud of you yet. Got any more?"

Roldan related the tale of Rafael's prowess with the bull, his own encounter with the bear, and Adan's timely interference. Hill then shook the hands of the two other boys, and told them that as long as he had a roof above his head they could share it, and that he'd do anything to help them but steal horses, so help him Bob. Roldan then told the tale of the earthquake and stampede.

"Ugh!" exclaimed Hill, with a shudder. "That's one thing I can't abide - your earthquakes. I tell you it's enough to take the grit outen a grizzly to hear the land sliden on the mountain and the big redwoods that has got their roots about the bed-rock come roarin' down.

When an earthquake comes I go and stand in the middle of the creek so as I can see what's comin' all round. Once I was on the side of the mountain when one of those shakes come and I slid down twenty feet before I could stop myself. It's just the one thing that has happened to me that I can't help thinkin' about. Well, what kin I do for you? You're welcome to stay here, but this hut ain't no great shakes for such as you. Be you goin' home, now that the conscription's over?"

"No!" said Roldan, emphatically, "we are not. There are other reasons why we must go to Los Angeles as quickly as we can. Could you get us three horses?"

"I could get them from the priest -"

"No! no!"

"Why, what's the row with the priest? Got in his black books? I shouldn't like to do that myself."

"You said just now that you would do anything for us. Would you even hide us from the priest if he came here?"

"I would. And I ain't the one to ask questions. If you don't want to see the priest, it's not Jim Hill that will assist him to find you. Been there myself."

"Couldn't you get us three horses from my father's corral - the Rancho Encarnacion?" asked Rafael.

"I could, if you'd go with me; but horse-stealing is just the one thing I agreed not to do."

"You might go with him, Rafael," said Roldan. "You

would get there after dark if you started now; and even if the vaqueros were not asleep they would not call your father."

"And I could send a message to my parents," said Rafael, eagerly. "Then they would not worry. Yes, I will go. The priest would not dare to harm me while I was with the Senor Hill."

"Oh, the two of us would be a match for even him, if it came to that," said Hill. "Well, we'll start right now, there bein' no call for delay. We'll have to foot it, as my mustang's laid up. If the priest should turn up here - which ain't likely - jest run up that ladder inter the garret and pull it after yer. Well, hasta luego, as they say in these parts. Make yourselves ter home."

XX

"Now," said Roldan, as Rafael and Hill trudged into the perspective of the canon, "we must sleep, but by turns. That priest will surely go to the cave to-day, and when he finds us gone he'll come straight for the mountains; and not through the tunnel either; he'll come on that big brown horse of his. You sleep first, for two hours, and I'll watch -"

"You first, my friend - " Suppressing a mighty yawn.

"It is easier for me to keep awake. Lie down on that horrible bed. I do not so much mind waiting a little longer."

Adan lifted his nose at the bunk covered with a bearskin, then flung himself upon it, and was asleep in three minutes. Roldan sat with his eyes applied to a rift between the hide-door and the wall. It commanded a view of the opposite wall of the canon, over which wound a zig-zag horse trail.

The sun, which had hung directly above the canon when Hill and Rafael departed, had slid toward the west, leaving the canon cold and dark again, and Roldan was about to call Adan, when he sprang to his feet, and stood rigid, cold with fear.

Gertrude Atherton

On the brow of the wall opposite, three hundred feet above his head, stood a powerful brown horse. On him was a huge figure clad in a brown cassock, the hood drawn well over the face. It was impossible to distinguish features at that distance, but Roldan fancied that those terrible eyes were holding his own. He recovered himself and dragged Adan out of bed.

"The priest!" he said. "Help me to wash these dishes - quick. It will take him some time to get down."

Adan stumbled across the room, plunged the dishes into a pail of drinking water, then handed them to Roldan, who dried them hastily and piled them on the shelf. Then he flung the water across the clay floor of the hut.

"Get up the ladder," he commanded. Adan scrambled up. Roldan followed, and pulled the ladder after him. The garret was very low, and half full of skins. They could not stand upright. It was also bitterly cold. Each hastily wrapped a skin about his body, and lay full length, Roldan on his face, his eyes applied to a chink in the rough floor.

A few moments later the door was flung aside and the priest strode in.

Roldan shuddered, but not with personal fear. The priest looked like a man who had just left the rack of his native Spain. His hair - the hood had fallen back - stood on end, his face and tightened lips were livid, his eyes rolled wildly.

"Jim!" he said hoarsely. "Jim!"

He left the hut as abruptly as he had entered it.

"He has gone to look at the mouth of the tunnel," whispered Roldan. "What fools we were not to cover it up again. Then he would have walked its length to find us, and the horses might have come before he returned. Well, he cannot get us until he pulls the roof down."

"He could do it," whispered Adan, grimly. "Those hands! Dios de mi alma!"

"He will think we have gone somewhere with Don Jim."

The priest returned in less than half an hour. His face, if anything, was still more terrible to look upon. There was a touch of foam on his lips. His great hands were clinched. He strode over to the bunk and lifted the heaped-up bearskin. Suddenly he pressed his face into the fur.

"Perfume - Dona Martina's," he exclaimed. "They have been here."

He raised his face to the ceiling, and the boys held their mouths open that their teeth might not clack together. They closed their eyes: instinct bade them give heed to visual magnetism. Roldan immediately wanted to cough, Adan to scratch his nose. The next few moments were the most agonised of their lives. They felt the priest lift his hands and pass them slowly along the ceiling, they felt those eyes searching every crevice. Then they felt him grip the edge of the aperture and lift himself until his eyes were above the garret floor. But it was pitch dark. He could not even see the ladder, much less the boys under the bear skins.

The priest dropped to the floor and seated himself upon a box, dropping his face into his hands. There he sat, motionless, for hours. The boys buried their heads in the skins and went to sleep.

They were awakened by the sound of voices. A candle flared below. Hill had entered. He and the priest were alone.

"They were here, sir, that's true enough. I've just taken them to the Sennor Carriller's and pointed them fur home. They seemed in a hurry to vamos these parts."

The priest groaned and struck his fist on the table. "Then they are leagues away by this."

"They be, for a fact. Their horses was fresh and they was powerful keen. They was just sweaten' to git home."

"And Rafael Carillo? Did he go with them?"

"He didn't. He allowed to, but his father warnt agreeable. In fact he was - savin' your grace - cussed disagreeable. He corralled us as we was corrallen the horses; and although he was mighty mad at such French leave, he said, speakin' of the other two kids, that they could take the two horses and git, and the sooner the better, and if they never come lookin' for adventures in these parts agin the better he'd be pleased."

The priest did not appear to doubt him. He was looking through the doorway. Roldan could not see his face, but he saw the stare of wonder on Hill's.

"Very well," said the priest, after a moment, and his voice was hardly audible. "I shall return now. Can you come down to the Mission to-morrow - no, the day after. I have a secret to confide to you, and it will not be to your disadvantage to know it. I had no intention of telling any one, but I need help, and now more than ever. There is no time to be lost. Can you come early?"

"I'll be there between dawn and ten o'clock."

"That will do. Good night." And the priest went out.

No one spoke until the sound came up to them of a horse fording the creek. Then Hill said cautiously, -

"Hi, there, young uns."

"In the name of Mary let us come down, Don Jim," hissed Roldan, through the crack.

"Well, I guess you kin. He's climbin' the hill, and I don't see as there's anything to bring him back. I hope the fleas ain't et ye alive."

The boys lowered the ladder as rapidly as their stiff fingers would permit, and a moment later stood on the floor of the room, shaking themselves vigorously.

"Where's Rafael?" demanded Roldan.

"Tucked in his little warm bed with a warmer hide, I guess. The old man caught us in the very act of horse stealin'. Holy smoke, but he did cuss. I ain't got no pride in Yankee cussin' left."

"What did Rafael tell him?" interrupted Roldan, eagerly.

"He told him as how he had made up his mind to go home with you for a little paseo -"

"Did he say nothing about the priest?"

"Nothin'. Never opened his head about the priest -"

"When I'm governor I'll reward him," said Roldan, warmly.

"When you're President of the United States you might make him Secretary of State -"

"But the horses? the horses?"

"They're tethered just over the mountain. I suspicioned the priest might be here, seein' as you were expectin' him, more or less."

"Did Don Tiburcio say about me - us - what you told the priest?"

"He did, and more of it. He was as mad as a bear with a sore head. You see, he hadn't had no peace of mind for some hours, and as for the old lady I believe she's been havin' high strikes regular since breakfast. Now, I'm hospitable, but my advice to you is to git. Like as not the priest'll see old Carriller to-morrow, and then the cat'll come out. I kin git outen it all right enough - I'll say as how the old man didn't see you, that you were restin' on the other side of the wall. Like as not he'll believe me, but he thinks you're pointed fur home, and if he wants you badly, he'll follow. You'd better go

South fur a month or so and go home by barque. I'll fetch the horses down now and put them in my shed. That'll rest 'em a bit and keep 'em warm, and then you kin start the minute it's daylight."

"You have been a friend to us in trouble, Don Jim, and I shall never forget it."

"Don't mention it, Rolly, don't mention it. I kinder like excitement, when I ain't the hero, so ter speak. There's only one thing I've got to ask in return: Have you got a grudge agin the priest?"

"I have."

"Be you meditatin' revenge?"

"A Spaniard never forgives an insult."

"Oh, . . . have you got it in yer power to injure Padre Osuna in the sight o' men?"

"I have, and worse - for him."

"Don't do it, young man," said Hill, solemnly. "Don't do it. It ain't worth shucks to ruin a man fur personal spite. You'll find that out the minute you've done it. You'll feel small and mean; and if you want to be a great man - and I kin see you're ambitious - that ain't the way to go to work. Padre Osuna has his faults, but he's a big man; there ain't none bigger in the Californies; and he ain't the man to ruin, without thinkin' a lot about it aforehand."

"He insulted me horribly," said Roldan, shutting his teeth. "I will never respect myself until I wipe out the

Gertrude Atherton

memory of that moment."

"He lost his temper, I suspicion, and whacked ye, like
as not. Well, I'll admit that is hard on a don of your
size. But, take my word for it, you'll feel a sight better
if you mount the high horse and forgive him, treat him
with silent contempt. Nothin' makes you feel as good
as that. Tried it myself."

"I must think about it, Don Jim.'

"Well, do. And maybe you'll remember that I asked ye
as a favour to let the priest off this time. He's been the
best friend I ever had, and he's been the friend of
many, young 'un."

Roldan stepped forward impulsively and grasped Hill's
hand. "I will never speak," he said. "And you can say
to Rafael that I wish him never to speak, either. Only,
in return, Don Jim, I insist that you do not tell him that
I promised you this. He shall not think that I fear him."

"Oh, I ain't goin' to have no conversation with him on
the subject. Don't you worry about that. Now, I'll go
after the mustangs. You lie down, and when I come
back I'll cook that there rabbit for yer. You kin git
dinner at the Ortegas', but don't stay there too long, for
the priest's mighty sharp."

XXI

The boys were once more adrift in the wilderness. It was with mixed emotions that they said good-bye to the hospitable American and rode forth to new experiences and dangers. They were now tried adventurers; they knew their mettle; they also had a far more definite idea of what danger and experience meant than when they had fled from home with the light heart of ignorance. Roldan felt several years older, and Adan had moments of reflection. Moreover, the fine point of novelty had worn toward bluntness. Nevertheless, they felt no immediate desire to return to leading strings, and were glad of an excuse to pursue their way south. Los Angeles was a famous city, the rival of Monterey, - which neither had seen, - and a fitting climax to an exciting volume. The exact arrangement of that climax was compassed by the imagination of neither.

For two miles they kept in line with the foot-hills, then rode rapidly toward the valley, impatient for its warmth. So far, barring their sojourn in the Sierras, they had been favoured with fine weather; but winter was growing older every day, and the sky was thick and grey this morning.

The Casa Ortega stood on the shores of a large lake. The banks were thickly wooded. On its southern curve

Gertrude Atherton

was a high mountain. As the boys approached, a vaquero sprang upon a mustang and rode toward them rapidly. Roldan recognised one of the men that had been at the rodeo.

"At your feet, senores," said the vaquero. "The Senor Don is away, and all the family; but I am mayor domo, and in his absence I place the house at your disposal."

"My father will reward you," said Roldan, graciously. "We would ask that you give us dinner, a thick poncho each, for I fear that it will rain before we reach Los Angeles, and that you will direct us which way to go. The ponchos shall be replaced with fine new ones as soon as we have returned home."

"Don Carlos would not hear of the return of the ponchos, senor. But surely the senores will remain a few days, until the storm is over?"

"We dare not. But we will rest; and we have good appetites."

The mayor domo, still protesting, held the horses while the boys dismounted, then showed them to two bedrooms and bade them rest while dinner was preparing. "It will be an hour," he said "I beg that the senores will sleep."

The boys did sleep, and it was two hours before they were called. Then they ate a steaming dinner, and forgot their fear of the priest: the meagre diet of squirrel and rabbit of the past thirty-six hours had lowered their spirits' temperature.

When they left the room the mayor domo awaited them

with two thick woollen ponchos - large squares of cloth with a slit in the middle for the head.

"These will keep the rain out," he said, as he slipped them over the boys' heads. "And there is food for two days in the saddle-bags, and pistols in the holsters. Keep to the right of the lake, and enter the mountains by the horse trail. It winds over the lower ridges. The senores cannot lose themselves, for they should be on the other side before dark - that mountain is the meeting of the two ranges and beyond there are no more for many leagues. Then the senores must keep straight on, straight on - never turning to the left, for that way lies the terrible Mojave desert. By-and-by they will cross a river, and after that Los Angeles is not far. Between the mountain and the river is an hacienda, where they will find welcome for the night."

Roldan thanked him profusely, then said: "I have reasons for not wishing ANY ONE to know that I have not returned to my father's house. I beg that you will tell no one, not even a priest, that we have been here, for three days at least."

"The senor's wishes shall be obeyed. The Senor Don returns not for a week. No one shall know until then of the honour that has been done to his house."

The boys rode rapidly through the wood over a broad road that had evidently been traversed many times. The sky was leaden, but no rain fell. Nor was there any wind. The lake could not have been smoother were it frozen, although it reflected the grey above. Wild ducks and snipe broke its monotony at times, now and again a jungle of tules. In less than an hour the travellers were ascending the mountain by easy grades, a black forest of pines about them. It was darker here, but the road was clearly defined, and they talked gaily of adventures past and to come. In Los Angeles they had many relatives, and they knew that a royal welcome would be given them. They would see the gay life of which they had heard so much from their brothers; and they magnanimously resolved that after a week of it they would return to their anxious parents.

"Ay!" exclaimed Adan, interrupting these pleasant anticipations, "it rains at last."

A few drops fell; then the rain came with a rush. For some time the wind had been rising; suddenly it seemed to leap upward to meet the emptying clouds, then filled the pine-tops with a great roar, rattling the hard branches, bending the slender trunks. The boys were on the down grade, and there was no danger of losing the path, although the rain had put out the sallow flame of the sun. They pricked their horses and made the descent as rapidly as possible. But it was another hour before they were on level ground once more. The rain was still falling in torrents; the wind flung it in their eyes as fast as they dashed it from their lashes. They could not see a yard ahead. The light of the hacienda was nowhere visible. If its owner was away from home and his house in darkness, then was their plight a sorry one indeed.

"There is only one thing to do," said Roldan, putting his hand funnel-wise to Adan's ear. "We must keep due south until we come to the river. Then, at least, we cannot go wrong."

"And that river we must cross!" said Adan, with a groan. "Dios de mi alma!"

Roldan had great faith in his sense of locality, but in a blinding rain on a black night with a mighty wind roaring inside one's very skull, and whirling the heavy poncho about one's ears every few moments, it was difficult to preserve any sense at all. They galloped on, however, occasionally pausing to shout, straining their eyes into the darkness on every side. But nothing came back to eye or ear. Apparently they had the wilderness to themselves. There was no sign of even an Indian pueblo.

It was during one of these halts that the boys ejaculated simultaneously: "The river!"

"No," shouted Roldan, a moment later "it is only a creek."

"Are we lost?" demanded Adan; and even the loud tone had a note of pained resignation in it.

"No; I think this must be what he meant. Some of the low people say river for everything but the ocean. It is shallow, and we cannot turn back. Come."

They rode along the bank until they came to an easy slope, then crossed, and cantered on. In a very short time the storm was behind them and the stars burst out, but there was no sign of habitation. They kept on for an hour longer, hoping for a welcome twinkle below; but not even a coyote crossed their path. As far as they could see in the starlight they were on a plain of illimitable reach, bare but for low shrubs whose kind they could not determine, although once Adan's coat caught on a prickly surface. The atmosphere was warm and very dry.

Finally Roldan reined in.

"We must rest," he said, "and build a fire, or we shall be stiff to-morrow. And it is long past the hour for supper."

"The sooner we eat and sleep and dry, the better for me," said Adan.

The boys dismounted and tied their horses to a palm, then looked about for firewood. There was not a tree to be seen; they had not passed one since they left the creek. Nor could they see any sign of flint with which they might set fire to a clump of palms.

Adan, who had been on his knees, suddenly remarked: "There is not a blade of grass, Roldan. What will the mustangs do?"

"They are eating the palm, perhaps that will do them until to-morrow. But the poor things must be as hungry as twenty. Come, let us strip, hang our things up, and run. The water is in my bones."

The boys peeled off the clinging steaming garments and ran up and down until hunger sent them to the saddle bags. The mayor domo had provided them abundantly, and once more they looked upon the world with hopeful eyes.

"But we must sleep," said Roldan, "and it is not going to be easy for mind or body - if there are rattlers about - with no fire. We must take it in turns. It is warm; we do not need our clothes - ah!" - for Adan was snoring.

Roldan was very tired but not sleepy. His brain,

indeed, seemed unusually alert, and he got up after a time and prowled about, pistol in hand. He had been in solitudes before, solitude of plain and valley and mountain; but there was something in his present surroundings that reminded him of nothing he had heard of or seen. It was not only the intense stillness, unbroken by so much as the flutter of a leaf, nor even the vast expanse. The place seemed to possess a character of its own, and its character was sinister and forbidding. Once or twice he had been in the cemetery of the Mission near his father's rancho, and the ugly feeling that he stood too close to death came back to him; why, he could not define. There was no sign of a cross anywhere; but he felt that he stood in a dead world, nevertheless. Once the ground quivered beneath his feet, and the horrible idea occurred to him that Southern California had been swallowed by an earthquake, and that only this desolation was left.

He went back to his comrade, who slept soundly beside the horses, also extended and breathing deeply. It was nearly morning when he woke Adan, so little aptitude had his brain for sleep. But when Adan sat up he fell asleep almost immediately, and when he awoke the sun was high.

XXII

Roldan raised himself on his elbow and looked about him. Adan was some quarter of a mile away, approaching him, leading the mustangs. Cleaving the horizon on four sides was a vast plain. On it was not a tree, nor even a hut. Here and there were clumps of palms and cacti, as stark as if cut from pale green stone. At vast intervals were short, isolated mountains, known in the vernacular as "buttes." On the ground was not the withered remnant of a blade of grass; but there were many fissures, and some of them were deep and wide. Of the things that crawl and scamper and fly there was no sign, not even a hole in the ground; for even reptiles must have food to eat, and there was nothing here to sustain man nor beast. The fleckless sky was a deep, hot blue; a blood-red sun toiled heavily toward the zenith.

"Adan!" shouted Roldan; he was suddenly mad for sound of any sort. A discouraged 'Halloa!" came promptly back.

Roldan dressed himself rapidly. His clothes were quite dry; indeed the very atmosphere of this strange beautiful place was so dry that it seemed to crumble in the nostrils. As he finished dressing Adan reached him. The horses' heads were hanging listlessly. Adan's face had lost its ruddy colour.

"Roldan," he said, "where are we?"

"I know not," said Roldan, setting his lips.

"I left you to look for water, and there are not even tarantulas in this accursed place. There is no water, not a drop. Nor a handful of stubble for the horses."

"We must go back the way we came, and start once more from the foot of the mountain."

"Can you remember from which point we entered this place? This soil might be rock; there is not a hoof-print anywhere."

"We should have gone south and we came east. On the northwestern horizon is something which looks like mountains - a long range - almost buried in mist. There is no sign of a range anywhere else; so the only thing to do is to go back to them; they are our mountains; I feel sure of that."

"If the horses do not give out. They are empty and choking, poor things. Well, there is no reason we should not eat, and, thanks be to that good mayor domo, we still have a bottle of wine. But I would give something for a gourd of water. However, we have not been girls yet, and we will not begin now, my friend."

The boys ate their breakfast, but their spirits felt little lighter, even after a long draught of wine. The awful quiet of the place, broken only by an occasional whinny from the mustangs, seemed to press hard about them, thickening the blood in their veins. Roldan was filled with forebodings he could not analyse, and strove to coax forth from its remote brain-cell something that had wandered in, he could not recall when nor where.

They saddled the mustangs, mounted, and were about to make for the northwest when Adan gave a hoarse gurgle, caught Roldan's arm, pulled him about, and pointed with shaking hand to the south.

"Dios de mi alma!" exclaimed Roldan. "It is Los Angeles. We were right, after all. But why were we never told that it was so beautiful?"

On the southern horizon, half veiled in pale blue mist, showed a stately city, with domes and turrets and spires and many lofty cathedrals. It was a white city; there were no red tiles to break those pure and lovely lines, to blotch that radiant whiteness; even the red sun withheld its angry shafts.

Roldan gazed, his lips parting, his breath coming quickly. If his imagination had ever attempted to picture heaven, its wildest flight would have resembled but fallen short of that living beauty before him. It was mystifying, exalting. It was worth the dangers and discomforts of the past month multiplied by twelve, just to have one moment's glimpse of such perfection. And it was Los Angeles! A city of the Californias, built by Indian hands! No wonder his family had been careful to leave its wonders out of the table talk; had he known, he would have been at its feet long since.

"It isn't the wine?" asked Adan, feebly.

"No. There must have been a fog before; Los Angeles is near the sea."

"Shall we start?"

"Yes, but slowly. The poor mustangs! But it will not be long now. We cannot be more than two leagues from there. See, it grows plainer every moment; the fog must have been very heavy."

They cantered on slowly, the mustangs responding automatically to the light prick of the spur. The beautiful alluring city looked to be floating in cloud; it smiled and beckoned, inciting even the weary famished brutes to effort. But at the end of an hour Roldan reined in with a puzzled expression. "I do not understand," he said. "It seemed not two leagues away when we started, and we have come that far and more, and still it seems exactly the same distance beyond."

"The atmosphere is so clear," suggested Adan. "But I wish we were there. My mouth is parched, my tongue is dry - and the horses, Roldan. Soon they will be as limp as sails in a calm."

"True, but we could easily walk the distance now. We could return for them at once with water and food." But he was beginning to feel vaguely uneasy once more. The odd sensation of death, of a buried world, had returned. Could it be that that fair city beyond was heaven? Surely, he thought with unconscious humour, it was very un-Californian.

They passed the lonely buttes, the parched beds of lakes, salt-coated. Still they saw not a living thing; still the city seemed to recede with the horizon, its sharp beautiful outlines unchanged. For some time the horses had been trotting unevenly. Gradually they relaxed into a dogged amble, their heads down, their tongues out.

Gertrude Atherton

Every now and again they half paused, with quivering knees.

Adan's was the first to collapse; it fell to its knees, then rolled over, Adan scrambling from under, unhurt.

Roldan also dismounted, and both boys, without a word, unsaddled the poor brutes, thrust the pistols into their belts and what was left of the provisions into their pockets. They cast off their ponchos, then once more turned their faces to the south. But they did not advance. They stood with distended eyes and suspended breath. The city had disappeared.

Adan was the first to find speech. "A fog?" he asked. "A rain storm?"

"There is neither. The horizon is as blue and clear as it is on the north and east and west. It is a miracle. Let me think a moment."

He sat down and took his head between his hands. After a while he looked up. "For hours I have been trying to remember something," he said. "Do you remember what that mayor domo said to us? - Keep straight on, straight on, never turning to the left, for that way lies the terrible Mojave desert, I barely heard his last words at the time; that is the reason I have had such a time remembering. We are in the Mojave desert, my friend."

Adan, whose mouth was still wide open, sat down and rolled his eyes from east to west. "Caramba!" he ejaculated finally.

"I could say a good deal more than Caramba. All that I

have heard of this Mojave comes back to me. There is no water on it, no living thing but half choked cacti and stunted palms. Men who are lost on it go mad and die of thirst -"

"Ay, yi, yi!"

"Si, senor. However, it might be much worse. It is winter, not summer, - when the heat kills in a day; we have food and a little wine; we are young and very strong; we have not come so many leagues that we cannot walk back. And we have each other. Think, were we alone!"

"Yes, it might be worse," said Adan, "but all the same it might be six or eight leagues to the northwest better. And that city? What was it? Where has it gone?"

"I do not know." Privately he believed that it had been a glimpse of heaven, and was disturbed lest it might have been a portent of death. But his mind was too active, his nature too independent to sit down under superstition. If he died on the desert, it would not be through lack of effort to get out of it.

He stood up, setting his lips. "Come," he said. "We gain nothing by sitting here, and we are both fresh; we can walk many leagues before night."

"Do you know which way to go?" asked Adan.

Roldan swept the horizon with his eyes. The buttes they had passed had displaced the solitary landmark of the morning. There was not a hoof-beat on the hard split ground. Roldan shrugged his shoulders.

"We can at least follow the sun. Los Angeles must be due west. Come."

The sun was past the zenith and sloping to the west. The boys turned their backs upon it and trudged on, only pausing once for a half-hour to divide the meagre remains of their store. Evening came; the sun leaned his elbows on the horizon in front of them, leered at the contracted visages and blinking eyes resolutely facing him, then slid leisurely down; and night came suddenly. The boys flung themselves on the ground and slept.

They awoke consumed with hunger and thirst. Their mouths and nostrils were coated with the fine irritating dust of the desert, scarcely visible but always felt. But their smarting eyes were greeted by a refreshing sight: not a half-league before them, directly in their course, was a lake, a lake as blue as the metallic sky above, and lightly fringed with palms and orange-trees. Beyond was a forest of silver leaves - an olive orchard.

"A Mission!" exclaimed Roldan, and even Adan sprang to his feet and marched westward with some enthusiasm. But alas! although they trudged with dogged persistence for fully a league, striving to forget the gnawing at their vitals in the exquisite prospect filling the eye, the lake seemed to march ahead of them, in perfect time with their weary feet. Suddenly the two boys paused and faced each other.

"This accursed desert is bewitched," said Roldan. His face was white, but more with anger than fear; for the first time in his life he realised the helplessness of man when at the mercy of nature, and he did not like the sensation. He had a strong, and by this time, well developed instinct to govern, to bend others to his will, and he swore now that he would walk out of this desert unharmed if only for the pleasure of cheating a force mightier than himself. He turned and looked at the sun.

"We have been going in a wrong direction," he said. "That lake has been shifting gradually toward the southwest, and taken us nearly a league out of our course. The first thing we know we will be in Baja California, where there is nothing but deserts, and they are all on mountain tops. We must strike north again. I am sure that last night we were due west of Los Angeles."

"But the lake? the Mission?"

"I do not believe there is any lake. There are things you and I do not understand in this world - although we are learning - and I believe that this strange desert has the power to make scenes like the theatres they who have travelled tell us of. Be sure that lake will disappear like the city."

They turned north in order to get in line with the sun; and out of the tail of their eyes they saw the lake march with them. When they finally turned to the west again it faced them once more. They linked arms suddenly and trudged on, hungry, parched, beset by superstitious fears, but not forgetting to turn every half hour and glance at the sun until he passed the meridian and pointed for the west. And suddenly the lake seemed to slip behind a wall.

"There is really something there this time," said Roldan, closing one eye and curving his hand about the other. "It is ugly enough to be real. It is no use to say how far anything is in this place, but I should think we would reach it before long."

And long before they did reach it they knew what it was - a thicket of cacti some two miles long and of unknown depth. The plants were eight or ten feet high, and the broad thick leaves, spiked, as only the leaves of the cactus are, looked to be welded together. But that was from a distance. When the boys reached the thicket they saw that the plants in reality were some feet apart, although there appeared to be no end to them. The boys sat down suddenly, their strength deserting them. They threw their arms forward on their knees and dropped their heads. For a half hour or more they sat motionless, then Roldan looked up and fixed his glassy eyes on the forbidding wall, which at close proximity seemed to girt* the horizon.

"If we tried to go round it," he said, "there is no knowing where we should find ourselves. We had better go straight ahead, if possible. If it is too thick we can turn back."

"At least we could not see this horrible desert for a while," said Adan. "I am willing."

"And, who knows? Los Angeles may be just on the other side."

Their utterance was thick. Their veins felt as if packed with lead, not so much from need of food as need of drink. But they stumbled to their feet and entered the cactus forest. They were obliged to pursue their way in single file; the spikes were long, and many of the larger leaves abutted so obstructively that they were obliged to go down on their hands and knees and crawl. Nor could they maintain a straight course, but zig-zagged among the great plants as nature permitted. More than once they heard the rip of silk, more than once blood sprang through their skin. Their progress was slow and fraught with peril, their only consolation that the end must come sooner or later.

Night came suddenly. They were near an open a few feet in circumference. They lay down side by side, knowing that a step at night might mean instant blindness.

The cactus never moves, not even in a storm. There was not a breath of wind to-night. The thick dull green plant-trees looked as solid as stone, a petrified forest. The sky had never seemed so high above, the stars so hard and bright.

Adan moistened his lips with his tongue. "Do you feel that you can last another day?" he asked.

"I expect to die of old age."

"Well, if you do, it won't be the fault of the Mojave desert. You have courage, and so have I; but this is worse than all - Do you feel that?"

"I have felt it many times before, to-day. It is said that parts of the Mojave shake all the time."

"We can swear to that. Supposing a great shake came, how could we get out of this?"

"We are as well here as anywhere. Let us sleep, and rise with the sun."

But although he spoke confidently, almost contemptuously, he was possessed with a wild desire to spring to his feet and fight his way out of this terrible prison. He had seen a huge fish flounder in a net, and looked on callously. He should never witness such another sight without a responsive thrill of horror. Were he paralysed from crown to heel he could not be more helpless in this thicket of needles. The vast unpeopled desert had been bad enough, but it had been intoxicating liberty to this. Tired as he was, he moved his hands and feet constantly; supineness was impossible. He wondered how men felt when in prison, and vowed that when he held the law in his hands he would invent some other way of punishment. For his part he would rather be shot at once.

Being young and healthy, he fell asleep after a time. When he awoke the sky was grey, the stars had gone. He shook Adan.

"There is no sunrise to be seen from this place," he said, "but I am sure of the direction now. I took note of that big cactus ahead, last night - Hist!"

"Dios de mi alma!" whispered Adan, his tongue rolling out. "In this place! It is worse than earthquake."

Nothing was to be seen from where they stood, but from no great distance came the faint hollow rattle which strikes terror to man in the wilderness. The volume of sound was suddenly augmented: there appeared to be a duet. Immediately it was supplemented by a loud furious hissing; a moment later by a whirr and impact.

"There are two, and they are fighting," whispered

Adan, his eyes bulging.

Roldan advanced softly to an aperture between two leaves of a cactus, then lifted his finger to his shoulder and beckoned. Adan turned mechanically in the opposite direction; but curiosity overcame him, and he joined Roldan.

Between two plants not three feet apart two rattlesnakes were engaged in mortal combat. They coiled with incredible rapidity, flew at each other with burning eyes and darting tongues, burying a fang somewhere in the tense bristling armours. The lashing tails struck the spiked surface of the cactus and augmented their fury; occasionally they whipped about, hissing deliriously, then returning as swiftly to the only enemy in sight. They had coiled and struck some four or five times, whipping all over their narrow arena, when as if by common consent, they retreated to extreme opposite points, coiled as lightning strikes, and leapt at each other. Even Roldan gave a hoarse cry of surprise, and as for Adan, he fell into vocabulary: one serpent had darted straight down the throat of the other. For a moment there was a fearful lashing. The choking serpent, with protruding eyes, like small green coals, and jaws distended in agony, strove to dislodge his suffocating enemy, and the other humped his back and leapt backward in frantic efforts to reach the air again. But suddenly their struggles ceased; they flattened to the ground, only the tails moving automatically. What was left looked like a monster of some unknown species; a creature with no head, a huge belly, and two tails.

"Caramba!" exclaimed Adan, "I could not eat that even if we had anything to cook it with. It looks like a mass of poison."

"I should like to know where that poison was last night. It may be a good sign, however: as they are the first living things we have seen, we may be near to the edge of the desert."

Adan crossed himself.

"Come," continued Roldan, "let us move on, before hunger tempts us too far."

Once more they started on their tortuous way. They walked very slowly, both from necessity and inclination: the excitement of the fight over, their physical necessities pressed heavily; they kept as close together as they could, but rarely spoke: they were too hungry. Both were oppressed by the fear that at any minute they would come upon a solid wall of cacti and be obliged to retrace their steps, and both knew that might mean a stunning blow to courage. At times the constant zig-zagging, the unalterable, smooth, grey-green surface of the cacti, made them halt dizzily, for both brain and body were sick for want of food. But by degrees the wood grew thinner and thinner; and when the sun was half way between the zenith and the western horizon, they left behind the last straggling outpost and found themselves on the edge of a creek, the same doubtless that they had crossed three nights before. They gave each other a feeble simultaneous slap on the back, gathered their energies, ran down the bank, and took a long draught of the running water.

"I feel better," said Roldan, finally, "but hungrier than ever. There are quail in that chaparral over there. I'll go after them, and do you hunt for flint and build a fire."

He crossed the creek and entered the brush beyond. Almost simultaneously there was a loud whirr of wings, and a large flock of quail rose from the chaparral a few feet ahead of him. He had only his pistols, but he was a good shot, and he decapitated two of the birds in rapid succession. Then he reloaded and killed a squirrel. When he returned, Adan was on his knees, with his large cheeks distended, coaxing a handful of dried leaves and twigs into flame. It was a half hour before the pyre was large enough for the sacrifice, but after that the birds and squirrel, which meanwhile had been skinned and washed in the creek, were but a short time singeing. It was an ill-cooked meal, but when it was over Roldan said solemnly, -

"I have eaten of all the delicious dishes of the Californias, including many dulces, but nothing ever tasted as good as this; no, not even the first breakfast at Casa Encarnacion."

"Nor to me," said Adan, emphatically, and he crossed himself.

XXIII

"Hallo!" shouted a peremptory voice. 'Hallo! Hallo!"

"It's the Senor Jim," gasped Adan.

Roldan sprang to his feet. "Hallo!" he cried.

There was a heavy trampling in the chaparral, and a moment later Hill rode into view. He took off his sombrero and waved it at the boys, but did not speak until he had crossed the creek and dismounted. Then he turned and regarded them with his keen hard eyes.

"Well!" he exclaimed, "I never calklated to see you alive agin, and that's a fact. Hed some more adventures, I presume. Look as if ye'd hed more adventures than grub."

"Indeed we have, Don Jim," said Roldan, solemnly. "Should you like to hear them?"

"Should I? Well, I guess. You and your adventures have kinder made me feel young once more."

Roldan told the painful story.

"Holy smoke!" exclaimed Hill, in conclusion, "you are tough! And two mirages in the bargain. I was lost on

Mojave once, and to my mind the mirages was the wust part of the hull game."

"What do you mean?" asked Roldan. "What are mirages?"

"Mirages, Rolly, are what ought to be and ain't, what you want and can't git, and they bear a hell-fired resemblance to life. I see you don't quite understand. Well, that there beautiful city and that there beautiful lake was what we call mirage for want of better name!" And he explained to them the meaning of the phenomenon, as far as he understood it.

"We have certainly learned a good deal since we left home," said Roldan, thoughtfully.

"There's room for more. There's room for more. Now, I suppose you'd like to know how I come here. Wall, I've got a confession to make fust, and seein' as you've been so nigh to death in the last few days, p'r'aps you'll furgive me. The day after you left I went down to see the priest, as agreed. I found him - well, I don't know as I'll tell everything, not even to excuse myself. It's enough to say that he was half luny between fear and remorse. He told me - I suppose he'd got to that state where he had to tell somebody or bust - about leavin' you in the tunnel to die, and bein' willin' after to kill you with his own hands - he was that mad. But he felt terrible sorry, and said that if you told on him it would serve him right; only that would mean ruin - ruin - ruin - a terrible word, young man. And he's not a day over forty and calkilates to git out of Californy with that there gold and be a big-bug in his native land. I hesitated some time, fur I ain't no slouch at keepin' a promise; but in the end I had to tell him. Why, a man's a criminal if he don't put another man out of misery when he kin -"

"You did quite right," interrupted Roldan. "I am glad that he was punished, but I would not have any one punished for ever."

"Well, I'm glad you feel that way. He felt good, I kin tell you that. He looked ten years younger in five minutes, for he said as how he knew you'd keep your word. I went straight off and managed to have a word with young Carrillo. It warnt no trouble to make him promise to keep his mouth shet; he's more afraid of the priest than he is of his father's green-hide lariat, and that's sayin' a heap. When I went back to the Mission I told the priest that I thought as how I'd go on to Ortega's, and see if you got there all right. When I got there and heard as how you hed crossed the mountains in a terrible storm I just hed to go on. I made straight for old Sanchez', who has a hacienda and raises grapes just this side of the river. He was drunk as usual, but his servants hedn't seen nothin' of you, and then I was seriously alarmed. That was at night, and I couldn't do nothin' until daylight, so I got a good sleep and the next mornin' I started for Mojave. I know it pretty well, and there was no danger of gittin' lost. At nightfall I found your horses and ponchos - the horses was dead, poor things. I slept on the desert that night, and the next mornin' rode back as hard as I could put, suspicionin' that you would have sense enough to strike west. I went round the corner of that there cactus wood, never thinkin' ye were in it, and I expect I got well to this side before you was out. When I got to this creek I rode up and down it, then crossed over, thinkin' ye might hev gone on. It was only when I saw smoke that I said to myself for the fust time: 'There they be.'

And you bet it did me good, for I was powerful worried."

"Don Jim," said Roldan, "you are a kind and good man. I love you, and I will always be your friend."

"So. Well, I'm powerful glad to hear that. You ain't much like 'Merican kids, but you're pretty clever all the same, and I like ye better 'n any boy I ever know'd, hanged if I don't. Don't be jealous, sonny" - to Adan - "I like ye too - but Rolly - well!"

"You would not like Roldan half so well if it were not for me," said Adan, whose face expressed nothing.

"So. Well. Now, be ye rested? We want to git to old Sanchez' fur a good supper and a soft bed to-night."

The boys rose with alacrity. Hill bade them mount his powerful horse, and walked beside them.

Sanchez' house was only three miles away, but the road lay through chaparral which sprang across in many places. It was heavy dusk when they emerged. For some time past they had heard wild eccentric cries, and their three pistols were cocked. As they rode through a grove of trees beyond the chaparral, they saw a dark something rolling toward them. In an instant Hill had snatched the boys from the horse and swung them to the limb of a tree.

"Hide yourselves among the leaves," he said, "and don't even breathe mor' 'n you kin help."

He gave the horse a sharp cut with his switch and it galloped on; then he climbed a neighbouring tree with

Gertrude Atherton

the agility of a wildcat, and crouched.

The boys gazed into the dusk with distended eyes. The cloud came on with inconceivable rapidity. In a moment it outlined itself. Those were living creatures, fleeing. A stampede? No, men. . . . What? Indians?

They were within a hundred yards now, and their lithe naked forms, the tomahawks and bows and arrows gripped in their clenched hands, could plainly be seen; a moment later, their evil faces, distorted with fear. In the middle distance behind them was a huge column of fire. A strange figure seemed leaping among the flames. It was from this scarlet column that the strange noises came. The Indians made no sound beyond their impact with the atmosphere.

They deflected suddenly and passed to the right of the grove; a moment later the three in ambush heard them crashing through the brush. Hill waited until the sound had grown faint in the distance before he swung himself down and helped the boys to the ground.

"That was a close shave," he said. "Them was murderin' savages, no weak-kneed Mission variety. I'd give two cents to know what scared 'em and what's goin' on over yonder. They were on the rampage, which same means thievin' and killin', or my name ain't Jim Hill."

"We're used to Indians," said Adan, with gentle pride.

"Oh, be ye? Well, if them Indians had caught you fryin' your supper, you'd have got as well acquainted with the next world in just about three quarters of an hour. Well, we've all got to foot it now; but it ain't far. I'm powerful anxious to know what's goin' on over to Sanchez'! Mebbe two tribes met and them's the victors offerin' up the tail end of that there valiant army. Golly Moroo, but they did look scared."

They walked on rapidly, but without further conversation; they were all hungry, and the boys were still very fagged. As they approached the blazing mass, the figure seemed to leap more wildly still among the flames, the cries to grow hoarser and more grotesque. All about was heavy blackness. The slender branches of the burning pine writhed and hissed; they might have been a pyramid of rattlesnakes caught in spouting flame. Overhead the stars had disappeared beyond a heavy cloud of smoke. It was a sight to strike terror to the heart of civilised man; small wonder that the superstitious children of the mountain and desert had fled in panic.

They had advanced a few yards farther when suddenly Hill flung himself on the ground and gave vent to a series of hysterical yells, at the same time rolling over and over, clutching at the grass. Roldan, seriously alarmed, and wondering if any other boys in the history of the Californias had ever had so much to try their nerves, ran to his assistance; he caught him by his lean shoulders, and shook him soundly.

"Don Jim! Don Jim!" he exclaimed. "Are you ill, my friend? You have some whisky in your flask, no?"

At this Hill burst into a loud guffaw. Roldan and Adan looked at each other helplessly. The Spanish do not laugh often, and although the boys dimly realised that Hill's explosion resembled - remotely - the dignified concession of their race to the ridiculous, yet they feared that this was a diseased and possibly fatal variety.

But in a moment Hill sat up. He wiped his eyes, and with some difficulty controlled his voice.

"No, I ain't ill, young 'uns," he said. "But them Indians 'ud be pretty sick if they knowed what they run from. That there object cavortin' round that there bonfire is old Sanchez, and he's drunk. Oh, Lord!" And once more Hill gave way to mirth.

"He did more good than harm to get drunk this time," said Roldan, smiling sympathetically.

"You're right, Rolly. You've got a long head. If old Sanchez had set down to supper sober to-night, there'd be a war-dance round another bonfire this minute, and his scalp 'ud be bobbin' bravely. I don't approve of liquor," he added cautiously, remembering the young ideas shooting before him. "I only said that there be exceptions to all rules, and this is one of them."

"I understand," said Roldan, drily. "I am not thinking of following the Senor Sanchez' example. But do you suppose that was really what frightened the Indians?"

"Just. Well, I guess! They've probably got some idee of the devil, and they thought that was him, sure 's fate."

He sprang to his feet, ran forward, caught the bacchanalian about the shoulders, and rushed him in the direction of the dimly-looming house, throwing one of his own long legs into the air every now and again. The boys ran after. When they reached the house its master was extended on a settee in the living-room, and Hill was telling the tale of their narrow escape to the frightened household.

"I don't think they'll come back," he said in conclusion. "But it's jest as well to have your guns ready, and for one or two of ye to set up all night. We three'd like grub and beds as quick as you kin git 'em ready."

Never had beds felt so sweet as they did that night. The boys awoke refreshed, themselves again; and no Indians had returned to disturb their slumbers.

XXIV

Hill met them as they entered the living-room. His eyes were full of news.

"Well, boys," he said, "I don't know that you're in fur another adventure, but ye kin call it by that name when you git home if you like; leastways there ain't no doubt about it's bein' an experience."

The boys forgot the waiting breakfast. "What is it?" they demanded simultaneously. "Quick! quick!"

"It's this. I don't suppose you know more about the history of your country 'n most kids do. Well, Alvarado and General Castro are your two big men -"

"We know that," interrupted Roldan, scornfully.

"Oh, you do? Then mebbe you know who'se* govenor* at the present moment."

"Micheltorena. He was sent from Mexico. People don't like him, and they despise the men he brought with him, still more."

"So. Well, I allus did say you was a remarkable kid, Rolly. However, this is the way the case stands now. Alvarado's mad as hops to be ousted for a furriner, so to speak, and Castro's been bilin' fur some time, because General Vallejo's been promoted ahead of him. So the two on 'em determined on a revolution. They had a skirmish on Salinas plains that didn't decide much, and then Alvarado and Castro marched south, from ranch to ranch, - you just levanted in time, - persuadin' the rancheros to uphold their cause and give 'em their sons. As they have a way with 'em, of course they got all the recruits they wanted, to say nothin' of the finest horses in stock - caponara after caponara. They say the sight when they marched into Los Angeles was somethin' to go hungry for. Of course all Los Angeles went over to such triumphant lookin' rebels, and to-day or to-morrow there's goin' to be a big battle. I only heard this mornin'. Old Sanchez' brother come post haste about two hours ago fur his gun and as many men and horses as he could drum up. Of course Alvarado marched down the coast valleys, so old Carillo and his neighbours are eatin' their breakfast in blissful ignorance."

"And shall we really see a great battle?" demanded Roldan, faintly. He was pale, his nostrils were twitching, "Alvarado! Castro! Micheltorena!"

"Well, you kin, if you bolt that there breakfast. The horses'll be here in about twenty minutes, and a battle's somethin' I'm pinin' to see, too."

The boys ate their breakfast rapidly and in silence. A half hour later they were galloping furiously for Los Angeles, escorted by the equally enthusiastic Hill. The river was low and quiet. The horses swam it without let from tide or snag. Even Adan forgot to cross himself. Beyond was the high hill that lies directly to the north of Los Angeles. Its surface seemed in motion; it looked

Gertrude Atherton

like a huge ant-hill.

"Them's women," said Hill, a few moments after they had left the river behind them. "Women and children. The fight must be on. Hist! Do you hear that?"

All three reined in. The sound of cannonading, distant but distinct, came to their ears. Without a word they lashed their mustangs and made for the city. They entered it in a few moments. It looked like a necropolis. Not a human being was to be seen. They spurred back to the hill and began the ascent, then paused for a few moments. It was a wild and tragic scene. Hundreds of women and children, their hair streaming in the high wind, were kneeling with uplifted crosses, praying aloud, when they were not weeping. A few men, Americans, were passing to and fro among them, administering encouragement; but their gaze also was directed anxiously to the north.

Hill dismounted and approached one of the Americans, conferred with him a moment, then returned to the impatient boys.

"They are fightin' in the San Fernando valley, three leagues to the north," he said. "We've got no time to lose."

They were less than an hour reaching the battlefield. During that hour Roldan scarcely knew how he felt. When he left the hacienda he was possessed by an intense curiosity only; but with that first dull boom something new and fierce had leapt to life within him. Every few moments his fingers moved round to the hip-pocket that held his pistols. The weeping women and children had made him quiver from head to foot.

As they approached the battlefield, and powder-smoke mingled with the green fragrance of winter, he thought that his nostrils would burst. His ear-drums were splitting with the thunder of cannon. Suddenly Hill caught him by the arm.

"Look!" he cried. "There be Alvarado and Castro over there, and Micheltorena on t' other side. Ain't they magnificent specimens? Why, what's the matter?"

"Let me go!" said Roldan. His face was deeply flushed, his eyes blazed. "Come, Adan! come, Adan!" he shouted. "An Alvarado! an Alvarado!"

"Holy smoke!" cried Hill. "You don't say you're meanin' to fight after sweatin' fur a month to git clear of the hull business?"

But Roldan, grasping the bridle of the less enthusiastic Adan, was already far ahead. The boys rode straight into the melee, firing through the smoke until their ammunition was exhausted. Even Adan after the first few moments lost all sense of fear, and following Roldan's example, snatched the gun from a fallen soldier and fired and reloaded until his hands were blistered, and his eyes half sightless with smoke.

Roldan, obeying his dominant instinct, pushed his way rapidly to the front, attracting much attention. Some one recognised him, and during one of the many pauses of this not very systematic and furious battle some one cheered the little don. The cheer was taken up vociferously. It boomed across the battlefield. A moment later a man came dashing across with a flag of truce: the cheering was supposed by the enemy to herald the advance of reinforcements. The truce was

Gertrude Atherton

accepted without explanations, and Roldan was hurried into the presence of Alvarado. That famous governor was sitting on a magnificent charger, caparisoned with carved leather, red velvet, silver, and gold. His black eyes were smiling, although the rest of his pale stern face was composed.

"So this is the runaway," he said. "I demanded you from your father, and he was much embarrassed to confess that you had fled to escape the conscription. Well, I am glad you did, for you have saved the day for me. But it is time you were in Monterey, for you've got the face of the leader of men, and the sooner your education begins the better. Will you come with me? Your father will not refuse."

The blood was pounding in Roldan's ears, but he managed to reply calmly that he would go.

He was then presented to General Castro, a man of fine military bearing, with classic features, but dark and stern. His eyes were as sombre as Alvarado's: doubtless both knew that their day would be short, their great gifts wasted in this far-away land, as remote from the great civilisations where lasting reputations are made as had it been on another planet.

He shook Roldan warmly by the hand, but he did not smile.

"Yes," he said, "it will be a pleasure to train you; and as you are young and malleable you will adapt yourself to the new order of things when it comes. Both Alvarado and I will write to your father; I am sure he will send you to us in Monterey."

And then they graciously dismissed him.

As the boys left the battlefield they came upon Hill, who was sitting on a hillock eating a sandwich. When Roldan had told his story the American replied:

"Shake! Rolly, you've got a heap o' genius, but you've got a durned sight more luck. You'll git there - one way or nother - if the skies fall. And I wish ye luck, I do for a fact."

"Don Jim," said Roldan, gravely, "have you another sandwich? We are very hungry."

Gertrude Atherton

www.ingramcontent.com/pod-product-compliance
Lightning Source LLC
Chambersburg PA
CBHW031346170626
46807CB00002B/858